MAGNUS FIN

AND THE FIN

SELKIE SECRET

MAGNUS FIN
AND THE FIN
SELKIE SECRET

JANIS MACKAY

 Kelpies

This book is also available as an eBook

Kelpies is an imprint of Floris Books

First published in 2012 by Floris Books

© 2012 Janis Mackay

Janis Mackay has asserted her right under the
Copyright, Designs and Patent Act 1988 to be
identified as the Author of this Work.

The publisher acknowledges subsidy from Creative
Scotland towards the publication of this series.

British Library CIP data available
ISBN 978-086315-865-0
Printed in Great Britain
by CPI Group (UK) Ltd, Croydon

I dedicate this book to all children who have ever felt, in some way, different. You're not alone.

Chapter 1

Waves high as houses reared, hovered then crashed, roaring onto the rocks. Salt spray spun through the air. Doors rattled. Chimneys moaned. Boats in the harbour were tossed high then flung low. The sea was a churning froth. Mighty waves smashed against cliff sides and hurled white spray high into the air. Magnus Fin was down at the beach watching, and yelling, and cheering. So was Tarkin, and they were both soaked to the skin.

Nearby, in the cottage down by the shore, Aquella sat in her room. With the window smeared with salt there wasn't much to see, but she could listen to the pounding, thundering roar of the angry sea. It thrilled and stirred her, but she was worried. Young seals could be dashed against the rocks. She hoped they'd keep away from the coast and stay deep. She kept away from the window, in case the storm shattered the glass and salt water landed on her delicate skin.

Magnus Fin and Tarkin, cheering from the safety of the heathery hillside, watched the sea fling scraps of rubbish onto the beach: plastic bottles, driftwood, branches, cans, ragged lengths of rope and unidentifiable flotsam and jetsam.

"Might be treasure in among all that rubbish," Magnus Fin shouted. He had to shout to be heard above the roar of the sea. His practised eye scanned the coastline. He could see planks of wood. They'd make a good bonfire, or maybe a bench for inside the cave. He spied a wellington boot, a yellow rubber glove, bottles, a car tyre and something blue that looked like a mangled tent. No antiques from the *Titanic* though. No treasure chests from sunken pirate ships.

A wall of water advanced. The boys staggered backwards, yelling as the towering wave crashed over the stones, flinging a heap of sand and a dark object onto the shore. Fin just saw it before spray from the mighty wave cascaded up the beach, drenching them.

Tarkin grabbed Fin's arm, screaming, "We could get smashed against the rocks!" He spluttered up water. "We need to get out of here. Fast!"

"But what about searching for treasure?" Fin pointed to the shore. "Something big came in. I saw it." Another huge wave broke, whipping their hair and lashing salt spray over their faces. Nowhere was safe. The wave's back-pull threatened to drag them both into the sea.

"OK," Fin cried. "Let's split!"

The wind tugged at them. Wet hair clung to their faces. Their feet splashed down into boggy puddles. As they ran, the small cottage close to the shore where Magnus Fin lived with his parents and his cousin, Aquella, came into view. From its stone chimney smoke puffed out and fled with the wind.

"You'd better come in and get dry," Magnus Fin shouted as they ran. "Your mum will go mad if she sees you soaked to the bone."

Two minutes later they were both huddled by the fire. Barbara, Magnus Fin's mother, flung blankets around them. She put mugs of hot chocolate into their hands, although Magnus Fin's were already warm.

"That's your selkie blood," Barbara said, rubbing his damp black hair with a towel. "But Tarkin," she moved on to rub his damp blond hair, "hasn't got selkie blood. Don't forget that, Magnus. Your friend is one hundred per cent human – aren't you, poor laddie? And you're freezing."

"I'll be f-fine. Honest," Tarkin stammered through chattering teeth. Then, as though wanting to include himself in this family of magical sea creatures, he added, "And I s-saw a mermaid once." Tarkin was convinced he had seen a mermaid on a fishing trip with his dad in Canada, and ever since he'd felt sure he would see her again one day.

Ragnor, Magnus Fin's selkie father who was stoking up the fire, smiled at the mention of the mermaid.

"I d-did." Tarkin nodded vigorously. "I r-really d-did."

Ragnor looked at this shivering boy with the long blond hair and pale blue eyes. "I believe you," he said, and smiled.

At that moment an almighty wave flung its spray all the way up the beach, lashing the living-room window. Everyone gasped.

Ragnor bunched his brow, the way he did when something worried him. "And I pity her out in this weather," he said, hurrying to the window. He could see nothing through the salt-stained window, but gazed anyway. "Aye," he murmured, "I pity them all."

Upset by the lashing wave, Aquella hurried downstairs to join the others. Magnus Fin looked up at her and grinned. "Hey, Aquella – it's totally wild out there. You should see the stuff on the beach. Something seriously big came in. Soon as the storm's over I'm going back to see what it is." Magnus Fin paused to gulp at his hot chocolate. "The waves are fifty metres high – they're huge."

"Totally awesome," added Tarkin, who had finally stopped shivering.

"And totally scary," Aquella said, plumping herself down beside the fire. There the three of them sat, staring into the orange flames, contemplating totally awesome waves and what that meant for the creatures in the sea.

"I hope the selkies are OK," Magnus Fin said. He also hoped, amongst all that flotsam and jetsam, he'd find something that could be called treasure.

Chapter 2

It's strange how an angry sea on Sunday can be still as a millpond on Monday. But strange things happen in the far north of Scotland, and not least of all with the weather and the sea. So it happened that the morning after the wild storm, Magnus Fin woke to the sun seeping into his Neptune's Cave of a bedroom, lighting up his driftwood mobiles, his shells, coloured glass, collection of bird skulls, bones and fossils. Had he dreamed the storm?

Seeing traces of salt on the window and the beach dotted with rubbish, Fin knew the great storm had been no dream. It had been real – and could mean treasure!

He fumbled in his drawer for his school clothes. There was nothing better than hunting for special things brought in by the tide, like dolphins' jaw bones or killer whales' vertebrae! He'd found a horseshoe recently and a shark's tooth. Shopping in town had nothing on beachcombing, and beachcombing was free!

In minutes he was dressed and, with a slice of buttered toast in his hand, hurried out into the bright morning. He set off along the beach path. Without meaning to, Magnus Fin found his steps falling in time with the lazy lapping waves. They were barely waves at all, more like tiny shifts in the water. Though he was eager to look for treasure there was something about the stillness of the morning that slowed him down. The sea swirled around the rocks, up the pebbled shore then back, sighing as though even that was too much effort.

It was hard to believe that only yesterday the same sea had been roaring, shouting, hurling spray high into the sky with foam coating the rocks and wobbling in the wind. Now it was still as glass, with hardly a breath of wind to ruffle its smooth surface. The birds that had somehow survived the wild storm of the day before were back, wheeling and crying in the blue air.

Magnus Fin studied the ragged tideline. Plastic stuff lay scattered amongst seaweed and stones. Fin knew it was rubbish. He knew it was ugly. He knew his father would probably come that very evening to clean the beach. But Fin also knew that amongst that rubbish it was possible to find wonderful things – things that had come from sunken ships, or from Denmark or Norway. He gazed up the coast, then down, trying to recall where the large thing was that he'd spied being hurled from the sea the day before.

Fin felt that rush of adrenalin he always felt when beachcombing. It was early morning. No one was around: only seabirds above him, the sea before him and the thrilling prospect of treasure waiting to be discovered. He ran along the shore, head down, pulse racing – but soon his steps faltered. Dead fish and dead gulls littered the beach, strewn and twisted among coils of rope and tangles of seaweed.

Anxiously Fin scanned the flat rocks by the caves, a favourite hauling-out place for seals. He dreaded the sight of dead seals battered by the storm. Seeing none, he turned his thoughts back to treasure. Where was the strange thing he'd seen flung ashore in the storm? Magnus Fin knew every inch of the beach so it didn't take long to find a big dent in the sand that hadn't been there before.

He squatted down and ran his fingers through the gritty sand. Three black cormorants stood in a row on a rock, their wings spread out – like washing on a line – to dry. Was that a good omen? Fin hoped it was, sinking his hands deeper into the damp sand. He liked the gritty feel of sand against his skin. He forgot about dead fish and dead birds and pushed on eagerly.

Everything was good, wasn't it? He liked being in Primary Seven and was excited about going up to the high school. His parents were happy. His selkie cousin Aquella seemed to be coping with human life since losing her seal skin. And he, Magnus Fin, had one green eye, one brown eye, webbed feet and was no longer ashamed of it. In fact he was proud of it! He liked who he was and, of course, it was the best thing in the world to have a best friend like Tarkin. He was so lucky, so very...

The tip of his fingers scraped against something hard. He stopped thinking and started digging. Whatever was in there felt cold and metallic. He dug deeper. Maybe it was part of the hull of the *Titanic*? Maybe he was about to get super lucky? Maybe amongst all these beer cans and plastic bottles there was some real treasure? By this time Magnus Fin had thrown back a mound of sand. The hard metallic thing, whatever it was, was big. This was surely the dark shape he'd seen flung from the sea. So he hadn't imagined it! He dug quickly, faster than a dog.

He threw up more and more sand, till he could run the back of his hand against something that felt like iron. He tried to push the thing but it wouldn't budge. By this time he had made a deep, wide hole. He lay flat on the sand and tipped his head and shoulders down into the hole. Pull as he might, the buried treasure wasn't moving. But what was it? A rusty chunk of iron? Gold? The skull of a blue whale? A bomb?

The three cormorants flew off. Still Magnus Fin, with his head down the hole, groped and patted. He couldn't feel an end to the thing. Maybe this really was the *Titanic* – the whole ship! How lucky could he get? Fin scraped his hands across the rough surface. He hit it. He punched. He felt something sharp. What was it? Still it refused to budge. Maybe this was hidden treasure snatched by a wave from a smuggler's cave? Fin's mind raced. His mother wouldn't have to take the bus into town every day to work – with this treasure they could buy a car. And his dad wouldn't have to work for the farmer all hours of the day and night. And Fin wouldn't have to keep his mouth shut when people at school went on about their holidays in Florida, and London, and Lanzarote, and Malta. Because with this treasure they could go abroad too! They could travel the world. They'd be rich!

Used to the shadowy light in the hole now, Fin could make out a kind of box. He peered at it and noticed a lid. He stretched his hands and tried to pull it open, but it wouldn't budge. He tried again, tugging at it for all he was worth.

Suddenly a blinding red light pulsed from the thing in the sand. Fin felt a searing pain shoot up his arm.

He screamed and yanked his arm back. He bolted backwards out of the hole. His left hand stung. He stared at it. There was a strange mark on the back of his hand. It was throbbing. A patch of skin between his thumb and forefinger was torn! The pain in his hand was hot, like fire. In horror he gaped as a drop of blood oozed from the wound and splatted down into the sand. He dragged himself backwards, staring in shock at the glowing deep red hole in the sand.

All the excitement turned to panic. What had happened to him? Fin scrambled to his feet, terrified now that some awful monster might leap from the hole, or an unexploded bomb might suddenly go off. The pain was unbearable. Through stinging tears Fin saw the hole in the sand pulse red then fade. It was alive, and it was warning him to keep out! Crying out in pain he stumbled backwards.

Cold water, that's what he needed. His hand was swelling up fast. He lurched over the sand and stones. He fell. He got up. He staggered down to the water's edge. He had his school clothes on, washed and ironed. His mum would go mad. But he had to soothe this burning hand.

He ran into the sea, splashing up fountains of cold water. Deeper in he waded, crying out in agony. When the cool water swirled round his waist he fell forward, submerging not only his bleeding hand but his whole body.

Like he knew it would, the sea brought relief. He lay under the soothing water, letting the lazy waves lap over him. A curious fish swam by, opened its mouth, then flicked its tail and swam off. Then a whole shoal of darting little fish came to look. With his green eye Fin winked at them. They shot away. Still Magnus Fin lay under the water, feeling the burning sensation in his hand cool down. The salt water stung the cut but at the same time soothed it. The thought of sitting in a stuffy classroom practising long division seemed like the most unnatural thing in the world. Fin, under the sea, was in no hurry to go to school.

He didn't have one green eye and one brown eye for no good reason. Green was for the sea; brown for the land. Magnus Fin, son of a selkie father and human mother, could breathe on land and under the sea. And that's what he did, while the water swirled around and above him, and the mysterious pain in his swollen hand eased.

Chapter 3

Mr Sargent was taking the register. "Saul?"

"Here."

"Tarkin?"

"Here."

"Aquella?"

"Here."

"Jess?"

"Here."

"Nasreen?"

"Here."

"Leo?"

"Here."

"Magnus Fin?"

"Magnus Fin?"

The whole class turned their heads to stare at the classroom door. Magnus Fin had an uncanny knack of appearing just as his name was being called. Even Mr Sargent gazed expectantly at the white door. But this morning the handle didn't turn. A skinny boy with a mop of black hair didn't fall into the classroom, out of breath with running and apologising for being late.

Mr Sargent glared at Aquella. "Well?"

Aquella, squirming in her seat, looked blankly up at the teacher. She twisted a coil of long black hair around her finger. "He went to the beach."

"The beach? Before school?" Mr Sargent shook his head and his ruddy cheeks wobbled. "Are you sure?"

"Yes. He always goes to the beach before school. To – um – see what he can find."

"Find?"

Patsy Mackay, at the back of the class, sniggered.

"Oh yes," continued Aquella, "you should see the things Magnus Fin has found. His room is full of selk—"

"Seldom found treasure," interrupted Tarkin quickly. He flashed a look across at Aquella and pursed his lips. Aquella looked down and said no more.

"So girls and boys," Mr Sargent boomed, "Magnus Fin hasn't come to school today. Magnus Fin will have the word ABSENT written in red pen against his name. And do you know the reason for this? Hmm?" He scanned the room, knitting his bushy eyebrows together and daring anyone to speak. No one did. "Because," he continued, his voice rising and rising, "Magnus Fin IS ON THE BEACH!"

Aquella gazed out of the classroom window. The sky was blue with only the tiniest puffy white clouds, a different world from yesterday. If she listened really hard she could blot out Mr Sargent. She could blot out the scraping sound of pencils being sharpened. She could blot out the sound of Sophie sniffing and Patsy trying to stifle a giggle. She could blot out all this, then she could hear the lazy swish of the waves as they curled over the rocks. She heard the gulls chatting down by the cliffs. She heard the shrill peep of an oystercatcher. And if she listened even harder, she could hear the seals sing and howl, far, far out at sea.

Then she had to hold on to the edge of her desk. She had to press her feet down onto the floor, to keep herself from running out of that classroom and down, down, all the way to the sea.

"Anyway, Aquella, your cousin might be messing around in rock pools or building sandcastles, but at least you are here – in school – where you're supposed to be."

Aquella tugged her thoughts away from her selkie family. She tried to concentrate on what her teacher was saying. He went on. "So perhaps you can tell the class what's in the news?" Mr Sargent fiddled with his bow tie and waited. "Well?"

"The – the news?"

"Yes, that's right. The news. Remember, I asked everyone to read a newspaper over the weekend, to watch the news, listen to the news. And I didn't mean..." He swung round to glare at Patsy Mackay with her plucked eyebrows and dyed blonde hair, "celebrity gossip, make-up, fashion, footballers' wives, talent shows and whatnot. Oh no!" Now he turned back to Aquella. "I meant – the news."

Aquella stared at her hands. She twisted her fingers together. Of course, there were things she could report. Like how her brother Ronan had won the selkie race to Stroma, and how just last week her grandmother Miranda had saved a stranded tourist, and how there were more storms than usual. And how selkies in the bay were already preparing for the summer solstice celebrations.

"I'm waiting..." Mr Sargent drummed his fingers on his desk. Tarkin coughed to get her attention. He'd already scribbled something about revolution in the Middle East on to a scrap of paper. It was now being passed under desks towards Aquella. "...and still waiting."

Aquella opened her mouth. She tried very hard to think of something. The sudden change in the weather perhaps? "Um..."

The door handle turned. News was suddenly forgotten. Everyone turned sharply to see a very wet Magnus Fin standing dripping in the doorway.

"Hi," he said, "um... sorry I'm late." Fin stepped into the class. A gasp like a gust of wind ran round the room. Everyone stared, open mouthed, at Magnus Fin's hand. He felt fifty eyes on him. The staring eyes burned him as much as the pain. He looked down. Part of his hand had turned a strange dark purple colour. It looked hideous.

"What the blazes?" shouted Mr Sargent, striding down the aisle of desks. Reaching Fin, he bent forward and stared at his hand. "Is this some kind of a joke?"

Fin's eyes fell to his aching hand, which Mr Sargent was gaping at. Fin sucked in his breath. He couldn't believe what he saw. Where he had cut himself the human skin had peeled off, revealing dark seal skin underneath. Fin pulled his hand away and hid it behind his back. Tears stung his eyes.

"I – must have – touched – um, something 'lergic." His voice wobbled. What was happening to him? What was happening to his hand? He shouldn't have come to school. He wanted to turn and run, but Mr Sargent had a hold of his wet sleeve.

"Allergic you mean. Well, that's what you get for messing around down at the beach." Mr Sargent frowned. He examined the hand closer. He stared at

Magnus Fin. He gaped again at the hand – the hand where an inch of dark seal skin had broken through! Gasping, Mr Sargent let the strange hand drop. He took a step back, flashing a fearful look at Magnus Fin.

"Ambulance!" he shouted. "Sophie! Quick! Run to the office. Ask Mrs Calder to phone for an ambulance. This instant!"

Sophie stopped sniffing and ran, circling Magnus Fin as though she might catch a horrible disease.

"No!" Fin blurted out after her. "No – stop." He plunged his hand into his trouser pocket. At the same time Mr Sargent grabbed hold of Fin's arm. "Please don't do that."

Tarkin and Aquella shot to their feet and called out, "No! Come back!" But Sophie was gone, slamming the door behind her.

Fin wrenched away from Mr Sargent's grip and stumbled for the door. With his good hand he yanked at the door handle.

"What do you mean – no?" Mr Sargent roared. "It's infected. I've never seen anything like it. You *have* to go to hospital."

But Fin shook his head. Salt water flicked into the teacher's face. Aquella was beside her cousin in an instant. Fin tugged the door open and ran. Aquella followed.

Spluttering, Mr Sargent wiped the water from his eyes. "Come back here," he bellowed. "You *must* go to hospital. Do you hear me?"

"But they can't. You don't understand. They can't go to a hospital," said Tarkin, then he too ran out of the classroom and sped after Fin and Aquella.

"*They?*" Mr Sargent shouted after him. "What do you mean – *they*?" He shook his head, stared for a moment at the retreating figures of Tarkin and Aquella, then ordered the rest of the class back to their seats. He groaned and glanced out of the window. Already he could see the flashing blue light of the ambulance in the distance.

Five minutes later Mr Sargent muttered his excuses to the paramedic. He was sorry – terribly sorry – after all it seemed to have been a false alarm. "The injured boy," he explained, "has gone!"

Chapter 4

No one likes to be made a fool of, least of all Mr Sargent. He was a great supporter of the emergency services and often went on about how anyone calling them out on false alarms should be made to pay. Now he sat at his desk in a mood. He had lost three children and it was only half past nine! He set the remaining children a very difficult long-division sum while he sucked on a barley sugar and tried to make sense of what had just happened.

What, he wondered, did Tarkin mean exactly by *they* couldn't go to a hospital. Just who were *they*? Unusual children were all very well. It didn't matter where they came from, what they looked like, what their parents did and didn't do. As far as Mr Sargent was concerned they were all children who would benefit greatly from school.

He chewed the end of his pen, and considered. There was unusual, and there was *very* unusual. And let's face it, he mused, there was something very unusual about Magnus Fin. Mr Sargent twiddled the ends of his moustache. Thinking of the dark skin he'd glimpsed, he frowned. Unless his mind was playing tricks he had seen thick hairs sprouting from that leathery skin, hadn't he? How odd! How very – he unwrapped another sweet – very odd!

And what did Magnus Fin fear in going to hospital? The teacher sucked noisily on the sweet, forgetting his class. Maybe they had strong religious beliefs? Or maybe it was something else? What about his eyes? Yes, his eyes were – not quite human. He unwrapped another barley sugar. Maybe that boy had something he was ashamed of? Something hospitals might discover. Mr Sargent was excited now. He'd make a few enquiries. Ask around. A teacher, after all, has a right to know just *who* he is teaching.

"Can't do it, Mr Sargent."

The teacher looked up and seemed surprised to see a class of children sitting in front of him. "Can't do what?"

"The sum," said Leo, who was usually good at long division.

"Aha! The sum," sang Mr Sargent, rising to his feet and switching from detective to teacher in an instant. "Do it for homework then. It's a tricky one, that one. Anyway," he smiled down on them all, "back to the news." He scanned the class then fixed his eyes upon little Ellie Manson in the second row. "Ellie, tell us, what's in the news?"

Ellie didn't hesitate. She had read three whole newspapers. She had sat through the *Six O'clock News*. She knew it all.

Except Mr Sargent wasn't listening. He'd had his suspicions about Magnus Fin and his underwater extraordinary abilities. And then there was that cousin of his; a lovely girl certainly, but always with that strange faraway gaze in her eyes. And weren't they rather round, and large, those eyes of hers? Then there was

24

her singing voice. It would bring a tear to a grown man's eye. And there was that strange, rolling way she had of walking. And to think of both of them, living way down in that little cottage by the sea with no neighbours, well, that wasn't normal either. And what about that peculiar illness Magnus Fin's parents had suffered from? In fact, the more Mr Sargent thought about Magnus Fin and Aquella, the more he was convinced that they weren't normal at all. And that American lad who was always with them – Tarkin – with long hair and a shark's tooth round his neck, well, he wasn't much better!

"And the pound is worth seventy cents against the dollar."

Mr Sargent blinked.

"And fifty-five boxes of haddock were landed at Scrabster. Crab stocks are up on last year."

He blinked again

"And Caledonian Thistle beat Celtic 3–0."

Mr Sargent stared at Ellie. "What are you going on about?"

Ellie stopped. Her face flushed crimson. "The news. I – I was just going on to the farming."

Mr Sargent thumped his desk. "Not the whole newspaper." He sighed. "Just the most interesting bit. What's that?" He glared at her expectantly. "Well?"

Ellie bit her finger, frowned, then smiled and announced, "Cherie Swan is to get a million pounds to go and eat eels on a desert island."

Mr Sargent groaned. The children in the back row giggled. The teacher lifted his eyebrows. "Really?"

"Yes, really," piped up Patsy Mackay. "It's absolutely true."

A few other pupils chimed in with how absolutely true it was. Everyone except him, it seemed, knew all about Cherie Swan. Mr Sargent fiddled with his tie. This day was not going well. He stared at the class, wondering what on earth to do next.

Robbie Cairns came to the rescue. "Please, Mr Sargent, can we make get-well cards for Magnus Fin?"

"Excellent idea, Robbie," said Mr Sargent, "and I will deliver them personally after school."

So that's what every pupil in the class did...

GET BETTER MAGNUS FIN
MAGNUS FIN RULES OK
HOPE YOUR POOR HAND IS FEELING BETTER

...while their teacher sat back down in his chair, wrote an apology letter to the emergency services and polished off a whole bag of barley sugars.

Chapter 5

Magnus Fin ran like the wind. In all their races Tarkin was usually the winner but this morning Magnus Fin ran as though he had turbo-charge in his feet. Down the brae he sprinted then slid down the hillside, snapping bracken stalks and ripping his school trousers on thorns. In no time he was on the beach path. Behind him he could hear Tarkin yelling for him to stop. But whatever was happening to him was too awful. He wouldn't stop till he was in the sea. His grandmother, Miranda, the queen of the selkies, would help him.

He shot horrified glances at his hand, his throbbing, swollen hand. Dark seal skin had broken through between his thumb and index finger. Terrified he sped on, leaping over boulders, litter, dead fish and puddles till he reached the flat black rocks. All the time his hand burned with pain. The thing in the sand had done this to him. What was it? Fin felt a shiver at the back of his neck. He shot a glance down to the beach. The thing in the sand was still down there somewhere.

Magnus Fin reached the skerries by the cave, his heart hammering. He leapt over the rocks. Fin had seen the flash of horror in his teacher's eye. Before he had pulled his hand away Mr Sargent had seen the seal skin. Fin knew he had. With a horrible sinking feeling Fin imagined their selkie secret plastered all over Mr Sargent's newspapers. They'd make front-page news. It would be terrible. Then the selkies in the bay would go away, they'd have to. What about him and Aquella and his dad? They'd be put into a circus! They'd be paraded around like show cattle. They'd be laughed at.

By now he had reached the tideline and hoisted himself up to the high black rock, which jutted the furthest out to sea. From here Fin could jump and go through the door to the selkie world, leaving the nosy human world far behind. He kicked off his school shoes, yanked off his socks then curled his webbed toes around the edge of the rock. He looked at his hand and shuddered. The water looked soothing and inviting. The sea would be his hospital. Fin bent his knees and swung his arms back. "Here goes!" he cried.

Magnus Fin jumped into the sea. No sooner had his hand hit the cool water than he felt relief spread through his whole body. Down and down he went. He knew the route well. There it was, the shell handle, shaped like a sickle moon, against an underwater rock. Fin reached through the water, grasped the handle with his good hand and pulled. He knew that rush of water, that sound of thundering music in his ears. The door opened. The flash of emerald-green light meant he was through. He had made it into the world of the seal people – his people – the selkies.

There, at the other side of the door, looking calm and beautiful in the serene, clear water, was his grandmother Miranda, the queen of the selkies. This hope at least had been answered. The great silver seal swam towards him and with her flipper she gently stroked his head.

Then, as if knowing his trouble, she touched his hurt hand, and, in the thought-speak of the selkies said, *Ceud mile fàilte – welcome, Magnus Fin.*

Tarkin, panting hard, stood on the beach and watched Magnus Fin disappear into the sea. There was nothing to do now but wait for Aquella to catch up. There was no point in trying to get Magnus Fin back. He had gone into the selkie world and Tarkin couldn't follow him – even if he could swim. Not even Aquella could follow him there. She was a selkie – but a selkie without a seal skin – who was soon to be a fully-fledged land girl, as long as she survived another month with not a drop of salt water on her skin.

"He's gone," Tarkin said, when Aquella finally caught up with him.

"It's the best place for him," she said between snatches of breath. "Poor Magnus Fin – did you see his hand?"

Tarkin nodded, though the truth was he'd only caught a glimpse. It had seemed bigger than usual, and it looked bruised. "Weird," was all he said.

"No, Tarkin, it's not weird. You say weird when you don't understand something. He must have scraped his skin against rust. We selkies have sensitive skin. Look at me – one drop of salt water and my skin will shrivel up. I suppose you call that *weird* too?"

Tarkin shrugged. He felt shaken. There was something wrong with his best friend. The last thing he needed was an argument with Aquella. "No, you know I don't mean it like that."

"Well, don't say it then!"

The two of them stood in awkward silence, the beach at their feet a mess of rubbish and dead creatures. They gazed out to sea, to the place where Fin had vanished. He would be back soon, that much Tarkin knew. Selkie time moved differently from human time. Fin had told him that what might feel like an hour under water would only be a few minutes in land time.

Tarkin turned to Aquella then, gesturing to the strewn beach said, "Fin must have been treasure hunting I guess."

Aquella nodded.

"And hurt his hand somehow."

Aquella nodded again, but pursed her lips tight, the way she did when she was annoyed.

"Look, you're not weird, OK?"

Aquella flashed her round green eyes at him. "I know."

Tarkin shot a glance over his shoulder, back along the beach path. Taking a step closer to Aquella he lowered his voice and said, "But you've got to be careful. I think Sargent's on to your secret."

Aquella swung her head round, as though expecting Mr Sargent to come thundering along the beach path towards them. "What secret?"

"You know – your selkie secret." By this time Tarkin's voice was barely audible. "Didn't you see the way he looked at Fin? And you? He's always giving you the suspicious look. It's like he knows you're both – different – but he doesn't know how."

"You mean he knows we're weird?"

"No. Well, yes. *I* don't think you're weird. But, like, *he* might. And you almost said 'selkie' treasures. Not a good idea, Aquella. Sargent wouldn't understand. He'd have you on the front page of his newspapers."

Aquella looked miserable. She tugged to free the pleat she wore for school and let her long hair tumble round her face. Through the curtain of her black hair she gazed out to the listless sea. "Fin should be back soon," she murmured. "He'll know what to do. Come on. Let's hide in the cave and wait for him."

Tarkin touched her gently on the elbow. "Cheer up. I think you guys are great – you know that. You are the best. But, seriously, I think you need to lie low for a bit – you know, act as normal as possible." Then he winked at Aquella. "And I'm sorry for saying weird."

Aquella managed a smile. "Well, you're not exactly the most normal boy in the world. You've got long hair. That's not normal – for a boy."

Tarkin laughed and flicked his ponytail. "Tell you what, you go back to the cave and wait for Fin there. I'll wait here in case he gets into some kind of trouble. Plus I've got a good view along the beach, in case Sargent sends out a search party."

Aquella shrugged. "OK, and tell me, Mr Ordinary, is it alright for me to sing while I sit in the cave? Or is that too weird?"

"Sure you can sing, but maybe you should sing kind of quiet?"

Aquella gave him a sailor's salute then ambled off to the cave, leaving Tarkin alone on the beach. He ran onto the rocks and from there scrambled over the skerries. Tarkin peered down into the glassy water, trying to catch a glimpse of Magnus Fin, but saw only his reflection staring back at him. The water was like a mirror; it was so clear Tarkin could see his blue eyes. He could see his shark's tooth necklace and his silver hooped earrings. When the wind ruffled the surface of the water his face wobbled, till he had several dancing eyes, and his chin flipped back and forth.

Aquella was singing an old Gaelic song about a fisherman who brought up a girl in his net. From the cave her lulling words drifted down. Tarkin felt he could stay there for ever, gazing into the water with the sun on his back and the song floating around him. Deep down, normal was the last thing he wanted to be, but he'd been called enough names in his life to know how badly that hurt, and he didn't want his selkie friends to suffer. It was hard enough for them – making out they were like everyone else, when half of them belonged under the sea.

Tarkin stared into the still water. A pale face gazed up at him. At first he thought it was his own reflection, distorted by the water. But it wasn't. He gasped. He didn't have green eyes. He didn't have twisted sea grass and cowrie shells in his black hair. He didn't have black hair! The face in the water was the face of a girl. Tarkin felt goosebumps crawl all over him. He didn't want to shout out in case he frightened her. His heart hammering in his ribs, he moved, loosening a pebble that rolled into the water. The glint of a fish tail flicked out of the water. When the water cleared, the face of the girl – and the silvery-blue fish tail – were gone.

It was his mermaid; he was sure it was. She had come all this way to find him. Tarkin ran from one side of the rocks to the other, scanning the water. Maybe she had gone round the other side? But only his face stared up at him. He ran to the cave and, throwing normality to the wind, shook Aquella on the shoulder. She stopped singing and stared up at him.

Hardly able to get the words out, his face flushed, his blue eyes wide, he stammered, "I – I – I saw her."

"Who did you see?" Aquella asked.

"My mermaid."

Chapter 6

Deep under the sea Magnus Fin, with Miranda close by his side, swam over the ribbed sand, over rocks and lobster creels, over rotting anchors, over a sunken ship, and on to the deep northern kelp forest.

Kelp will heal your hand, Miranda said as they swam. *We seal people have used kelp for centuries. You know, when I was a pup my mother wrapped me in kelp. She said it would give me special powers and keep me safe. That was a long, long time ago and I'm still here, so I think it worked.*

As they swam Magnus Fin listened. He didn't know his grandmother was keeping him distracted with her stories. She could see his swollen hand. She could see his seal skin breaking through. She knew they had to hurry. She also knew it wasn't ordinary rust that had caused such a strange reaction. She was worried, but tried not to show it. So she chattered, and Fin, happy to listen, forgot his pain and thought instead about a young seal wrapped in bandages of seaweed.

She said if I was to grow up strong and be a leader for the selkie people I would need to make friends with kelp. I didn't like the taste at first. I preferred a good fat salmon, but my mother insisted I try her kelp soup.

On and on they swam. The sea seemed murky, flat and gloomy. As Magnus Fin cast his eyes about him, the destruction after the storm was evident. He spied smashed lobsters, broken creels and everywhere a brown haze. Miranda swam with her seal body pressed close to Magnus Fin, to protect him and keep him warm. Fin had jumped into the sea without his wetsuit, and a school uniform was hardly fitting swim gear for the cold North Sea, even if it was the month of June.

They slowed down when the dark swaying kelp forest came into view. *We'll have you on the mend in no time,* Miranda said, flicking her body to glide downwards. She nudged Fin along with her, then, when they reached the slow swaying tops of the seaweed, left him and dived down amongst the dark fronds.

Fin treaded water and watched as Miranda, with lightning speed, pulled up strand after strand of the best kelp, using her flashing teeth and her deft flippers. She tore strands free of their holdfasts, and when she had finished looked like some storybook creature – a silver seal with a long wavy beard. Fin laughed at the sight, but catching the flicker of fear in Miranda's eyes, his laughter quickly died away.

We have to act fast, she said, nuzzling him out of the kelp forest and on into the still waters of a nearby cavern. Glancing about, Fin saw stones arranged like seats and tables. Miranda nudged Fin gently down onto a flat stone that looked like a table and there she wrapped the kelp bandages around his hand. Instantly Fin felt the effect. The seaweed seemed to suck the burning from him. He could feel his torn skin close up.

It was only when the bandage was secured that Miranda allowed herself to slump down onto the flat rock beside her grandson and rest. She looked into his eyes, concern shadowing her beautiful face. *We are lucky the kelp still contains healing power. So much is losing its power. You must have noticed – all is not well in the sea. What happened, Magnus Fin? Tell me, what did you touch?*

It seemed a long time ago. Fin tried to reach for the memory. There had been damp, gritty sand. And a storm. And rubbish. He had been excited. Treasure. He had discovered something. But what was it? *I don't know,* was all he could say.

Try and remember, Fin. These are uncommon tides, uncommon times. Angry storms one day, flat tired seas the next. Please, Fin – this is important. What happened?

He stared at his hand, now fat with seaweed bandages. Slowly it came to him. *It was a thing washed up in the storm,* he said.

What kind of a thing?

I don't know.

Just then a luminous jellyfish drifted into the cavern, stretching its long tendrils. It seemed surprised to find a silver seal and a boy resting in there. Shaking out its many tentacles it turned and floated away.

Neptune whipped up a storm to clear the seas, Miranda said. *He does that often now, as though he's angry. There's a lot of rubbish in the ocean and Neptune doesn't like that.*

I bet he doesn't, Fin said, remembering the one time he had met the mighty King Neptune. The image of him waking from the long sleep inflicted upon him by the monstrous false king, then rising from that great bed of shells, his long hair like a mighty kelp forest, his magnificent sea-green skin and deep kind eyes, would be with him for ever.

But he will be sad to think that in clearing the ocean he caused you pain.

Fin smiled at his grandmother. With the kelp bandage tight around his hand he felt no pain. Even the memory of the pain was gone. It would, he felt, be a good thing to stay in this peaceful sea cavern, with his grandmother by his side and the occasional visiting jellyfish, for a long, long time.

But Miranda had a different idea. She raised her head and nudged him. With a quick movement she pulled off the bandage with her teeth, examined his hand then said, *It has worked. There is still – thank Neptune – some goodness in the sea. Now it's time to take you back to the land. We don't want to be here when another storm rages. Come, Magnus Fin! And whatever that thing in the sand is – and I will try and find out what it is – don't touch it.*

Miranda guided Fin up from the stone table. Together they floated through the water and out of the quiet cavern. As they swam through the strangely listless sea she told him, *After Neptune's sea-storms unusual things can happen. Creatures can cover great distances with the force of the ocean swell. Objects, buried for centuries, can end up in different continents. We selkies stayed safe in the cavern till the sea-storm passed. But beware, Magnus Fin, the deeps have been thrashed. The sea has changed and sands have shifted. All, I fear, is not well with our sea king.*

As Miranda spoke they swam over a bed of yellow sea anemones, where shattered lobsters lay, pincers severed from their bodies. *Aye look,* she went on, *while we selkies found shelter in the storm, others were not so lucky.*

On they travelled, over the kelp forest then over a sunken ship. A heavy gloom pervaded the sea, as though the sea itself was tired – spent after its angry thrashings.

Fin tried to slow Miranda down, so he could have a better look at the sunken ship. Through the green murky water it looked eerie and ancient. But Miranda seemed in a hurry. This was no time for explorations. She pushed him on. Fin grabbed hold of her flipper and travelled that way, like a streak of water lightning. Shoals of fish darted into the shadows as they approached. A wide-mouthed dogfish opened and closed its mouth. An eel uncoiled and flicked through the water, like a lasso. On they swam, passing flat fish, catfish, crabs and black fish.

As they glided into shallower waters and the scent of land was upon them, Fin remembered he had something else to tell his grandmother. *Miranda? I think my schoolteacher guesses I'm a – a bit different.*

Miranda swung round. She splayed her flippers and brushed his face with her long whiskers. *What?*

The words tumbled from him. *I think my schoolteacher saw the seal skin in my hand. I think he suspects. And he likes newspapers.*

By this time they had reached the door to the land world. Miranda hung in the water. Her words came deep and serious. *Guard the selkie secret, Magnus Fin. Otherwise you, Ragnor and Aquella will have no peace.*

Miranda stroked the rock door with her flipper. Selkies had been crossing this threshold into the human world for millennia. Miranda's beautiful eyes darkened. *With these moody storms of late many selkies feel safer on land. Many's the night, as you lie in bed and the moon hangs like a lamp in the sky, seal coats are discarded and selkies in human form seek safety in the cave. The land is also our home. But now, you say, even the land is not safe.*

Miranda fell silent then stretched her flipper and stroked Fin's arm. *For generations humans lived peacefully with selkies, but so many spurn us now. If our secret falls into ignorant hands only dear Neptune knows how we are to survive, and the sorry truth is, I am not sure even he knows now.*

Magnus Fin continued to tread water. He was in no hurry to return to a place where people might jeer and point fingers at him.

Go now, Miranda continued. Sensing Magnus Fin's reluctance she softened her voice and stroked his head with her flipper. *Be brave, Magnus Fin, child of both worlds. Give my love to my son Ragnor, to your dear mother Barbara and to Aquella. And please be careful. Now go.*

With that, Miranda flicked her tail fins, twisted round and glided away while Magnus Fin, with his healed hand, clutched the shell handle, pushed open the rock door, and left the selkie world.

Chapter 7

No sooner had Magnus Fin hoisted himself up to the black rock and retrieved his school shoes than he heard Tarkin's signal: three short whistles. Fin looked up. There was Tarkin, standing by the mouth of the cave, waving him over.

Fin made his way to the cave, a sense of dread hanging over him like a dark cloud. He should be feeling happy. He had seen his grandmother. He had been in the selkie world. He had seen a sunken ship. His hand was completely healed. He examined it again just to make sure; not a hint of seal skin could be seen. But Magnus Fin wasn't happy. Not one bit. Miranda, the selkie queen, had seemed ill at ease, and even the mighty King Neptune, she said, was unhappy.

Fin glanced back at the flat and lifeless sea then twisted his hair around his finger and sighed. All he had wanted was to find treasure and now he was trusted to guard the selkie secret. That felt like a heavy burden to carry. If the secret got out, the selkies would be in the news – and such news could change their lives for ever.

Reaching the cave, he immediately saw Tarkin's bright eyes flash to his hand.

"Don't worry," Fin said, waving his fingers. "It's sorted. I'm fine. I'm normal." Fin stared at Tarkin who was hopping from foot to foot, a huge smile on his face.

"But what about you, Tark? What happened? You look like you just won a gold medal or something. What's up?"

"You are so not going to believe this, Fin. I saw her. I seriously saw her. My mermaid. She made it to Scotland! All the way from Canada. Can you believe that?"

This was one thing too much for Magnus Fin. And anyway, hadn't Tarkin thought he'd seen his mermaid at least twenty times in the past year? He'd seen her in swimming pools. He'd seen her in puddles. He'd seen her in Loch Ness.

"That's great," Fin said, his voice as flat as the sea as he peered over Tarkin's shoulder. "Where's Aquella?"

"She's lying low inside. Fin, you gotta lie low too. I think Sargent suspects stuff. So I've got a plan."

Fin sneaked into the dark cave with Tarkin on his heels.

"You guys have gotta act as normal as possible. I saw the way Sargent looked at you – and it's not the first time. I know that look and I don't like it, not one bit. And now that my mermaid has found me, I've gotta act normal too. We're in this together."

"I think Tarkin's overdoing it," said Aquella from the back of the cave. "And I reminded him that he isn't exactly Mr Ordinary Boy, is he? I also told him his mermaid could have been a mirage."

Magnus Fin squatted down on a stone next to Aquella. Tarkin squinted to see in the shadowy cave.

"No, she wasn't a mirage, and no, I'm not Mr Ordinary Boy, and that's why I know what it's like. Really, guys, you gotta take me serious."

"What do you mean?" Aquella asked as she took Fin's hand in her own and checked his skin.

"Selkies – that's what he means," Fin murmured, pulling his hand back. "Sargent suspects."

"Correct," said Tarkin. "He might set a detective on to you. Scientists even – or," Tarkin lowered his voice, "the paparazzi."

Aquella gasped. "The papa what?"

Tarkin, glancing over his shoulder, repeated slowly, "PA–PA–RA–ZZI! Meaning photographers with big cameras that snoop on celebrities or, you know, folk that are different, like mermaids or selkies... get it? You know how crazy he is about newspapers!"

"Well, I don't get it," she said, folding her arms, "not a bit."

Fin, looking pale, said nothing.

"Listen, Aquella," Tarkin whispered, "there are a few things you gotta learn about being human. And if you want a good life, have fun and all that, you don't want to go around telling everyone you're a selkie. Believe me – they'd put you in a cage. They'd charge people to come and gape at you." Tarkin had forgotten his whisper. "Act normal – know what I'm saying?" Aquella nodded. Fin listened but said nothing.

"Anyway, I'm a land girl now," Aquella insisted. "I *am* normal. I can read, and use a fork and knife. I can almost tie my laces."

"You're doing great. You're seriously clever. But look – I don't mean to be rude – but you do, you know, um, walk kind of strange."

Fin twisted his lucky moon-stone that hung on a leather lace around his neck. Things were going from bad to worse. His hand had been bad enough. The gloomy sea felt wrong. The thing in the sand was awful.

The idea of snooping journalists was even worse. And then to think that the selkies might be forced to go away – that he might never see them again. And poor Aquella looked on the verge of tears...

Magnus Fin groaned loudly. The others stared at him. "I saw it glow!"

That stopped Tarkin going on about normality. "You what?" he said.

"I saw it glow. Really. I mean, it could be a mine-sweeper or a bomb. I was hoping it would be treasure. Another bit of the *Titanic* would be good. Or gold coins. But whatever it is, it glowed, like it was telling me, 'Back off!'"

Tarkin shot a glance outside, then back at Fin. "What are you talking about?"

"It was washed up in the storm. I tried to open it – it's some kind of box. It really hurt and it glowed." Fin's voice cracked. "Do you want to see it?"

Tarkin was usually up for any adventure. He'd risked his life on the sea for Magnus Fin, and there were many times he wished he too was a selkie. But now didn't seem the time to investigate a dangerous glowing box.

"Dunno man," he muttered. "The paparazzi might be out. I mean, we're supposed to be in school."

"Well, I would," Aquella said.

"OK." Fin stepped out into the sunlight. It dazzled after the darkness of the cave. "The coast is clear," he reported. "Come on."

Reluctantly Tarkin left the safety of the cave. Fin and Aquella were already hurrying ahead. "Hey!" Tarkin called. "Wait for me!"

The fulmars were out in force, wheeling and screeching in the blue air, but there was no teacher or snooping journalist. Relieved, the three of them ran over the sand. A minute later they circled the hole and stared down.

"Wow," Aquella said, "you dug all that?"

"Yes." Fin nodded, wishing he hadn't.

"It's deep," she said.

"Totally huge," added Tarkin.

It was. And somehow it seemed much deeper than it had been an hour ago. Fin stared down the sandy hole.

"Hey, buddy, thought you said it glowed?"

"It did. I know it just looks like a hole in the sand now. But honest, something down there glowed!"

They all bent their heads forward and peered down. Fin bent the furthest. Even though whatever was in there had hurt him, he was still curious. It pulled him like a magnet. He dropped on to his knees for a better look, but this time kept his hands behind his back. Some sand had slipped back in, half covering the metal thing. Fin wondered if he'd imagined the glowing bit. The sun was higher in the sky now and rays of sunlight fell down the hole. The rusty metal, Fin saw, had studs on it, one of which was ragged and sharp.

Aquella found a long stick on the sand. "Here," she said, giving it to Fin, "prod whatever's down there with this. But don't touch it!"

Magnus Fin stabbed at the rusty metal thing and cleared the sand off it. He poked it, trying to prize open the flat casing that looked like a lid. He jabbed it. The three of them, staring down, heard the thing clang as Fin hit it. Fin jabbed under the lid again and tried to

44

flip it open. Suddenly the metal thing glowed red. Bright red! Aquella screamed.

"Don't touch it," Tarkin yelled. "Just leave it." He grabbed Fin's sweatshirt and yanked him back. "Wow, this is way too creepy."

Fin flung the stick down. "I told you! It's alive!" His face had turned pale but he didn't run away. "It's a kind of box. I mean, it could be a bomb. Maybe it's – you know – radioactive?"

Tarkin had jolted backwards. He stood now, shaking like a leaf. "I've read all about bombs. That ain't no bomb. There's something seriously weird going on here. Listen guys, you gotta take me serious. Leave this thing alone. You gotta act normal. Want my advice?"

Fin and Aquella didn't say anything, but Tarkin gave his advice anyway. "Let's throw the sand back in, lie low in the cave, and cook up some story about your hand and why we're not at school. Then launch Mission Act Normal, OK?"

The glowing red light died down, but Fin still found it hard to pull his gaze away. He'd set his hopes on finding treasure, and now, even though the thing had hurt him, he couldn't convince himself it wasn't treasure.

"Good idea," said Aquella, "let's cover it with sand."

At that moment they heard a shrill voice ring out. It was a man with his dog, heading their way. In a flash Tarkin kicked sand into the hole. Aquella helped while Magnus Fin could only stare as the mysterious box – along with all his hopes of treasure – vanished.

"Quick! Back to the cave!" Tarkin ordered, and the three of them sped over the beach and slipped into the darkness of the cave.

There they stayed, waiting for the school day to be over, while lazy waves licked the rocks, while bats flew above their heads, and while the mysterious glowing thing in the sand lay nearby, buried but not forgotten.

Chapter 8

At half past three Tarkin – the only one with a watch – announced that it was safe to go home. Faint with hunger they slipped out of the cave and hurried over the beach, avoiding the frantically covered-up hole. Tarkin skirted the sea to take one more look in the water, but his mermaid, he reported sadly, must have gone.

"But she won't be far," he added, the old twinkle back in his blue eyes. "Like, if she made it all this way to see me, she's not gonna take off again, is she?"

Magnus Fin shrugged.

Tarkin pulled at his sleeve. "Hey, Fin, you're my best pal, and you don't believe me. That hurts. I seriously saw her. And yeah, I know I've said that before, but this time it's true. It was *her*. Your dad believes me." Tarkin forced Fin to look at him. "And you don't?"

Fin saw the intensity flash in Tarkin's eyes. He knew that intensity. Didn't he feel that way himself about the selkies? About King Neptune? About the so-called sea magic that was as real to him as bikes and skateboards are to other boys? He scuffed sand and kicked aside a Coke can. "I don't know, Tark."

"Well, at least say maybe." Tarkin, in the middle of the beach, sunk to his knees and did his praying act. "Please?"

"OK – maybe. Maybe you really did see your mermaid. Maybe she really did cross the Atlantic ocean just to see you."

Tarkin seemed satisfied. "Aquella, how about you?"

"I know a bit about mermaids. We call them the Merrow. When they want to they can out-swim a selkie, they can out-swim a shark. They often guide sailors through rough seas. Yes, I've known a few Merrow so I'll say probably."

Tarkin grinned, stood up and leapt over a boulder. "And I say definitely!"

They hurried the rest of the way and soon the cottage was in view. The sight of it, with its natural stone, its blue painted windows and little garden seemed to make everything better. They ran now and with every stride the buried thing in the sand seemed to drop deeper and deeper, like a dream does when you wake up – as though it had never happened.

At the garden gate they paused. "OK," panted Tarkin, breathing fast, "from now on it's Mission Act Normal. I won't doodle mermaids on my jotter; you two try to act like other kids. Agreed?"

Fin and Aquella nodded.

"Oh, and Fin, I've been thinking..." Tarkin grinned and winked. "Maybe you should wear sunglasses." With that he laughed and ran off down the track. Magnus Fin laughed too, picturing himself sitting in the classroom with dark glasses on.

"Sometimes," muttered Aquella, "I really don't know if he's being serious or not." Then she pushed open the front door of the cottage.

She and Magnus Fin stepped into the living room and had just opened their mouths to say "Hi" when they promptly shut them again, and gasped.

"Oh, Fin, Aquella, glad you're back." Barbara sat on the sofa, looking embarrassed. In the armchair opposite her sat Mr Sargent. He cleared his throat and drummed his fingers on the armrest of his chair. "Your teacher," she said, flashing them her what's-this-all-about look, "has just arrived. It seems he wants to talk to me."

"Yes, that's right, it won't take long. But it is – I'm afraid – rather," he turned to glance at Magnus Fin, who with Aquella stood huddled by the living-room door, "serious." Mr Sargent was obviously trying to get a good view of Magnus Fin's hand. Fin shuffled backwards. "How's the hand?" Mr Sargent called out.

Fin nodded. "Oh, fine. Yeah, turned out it was nothing. A wee sting."

"Nothing at all," chimed in Aquella.

Now Barbara was the one to clear her throat. She looked worried.

"I'm perfectly fine, Mum, really," Fin said quickly, by this time halfway out of the room.

"Good. I'm glad about that. Anyway, children, why don't you run off and do your homework? I won't be long."

In two seconds flat they were gone. But they didn't go far. They shut the living-room door, then hunched down behind it. Fortunately it was an old cottage and the door had cracks in the wood; perfect for listening in to adult's conversations. Mr Sargent's voice though was deep and it was hard to catch everything.

"It was – size of football – dark patches – he – afraid – the American lad, Tarkin – hospitals... I just – is there any special – your son – not – doctor?"

Tarkin was right. He's on to us, Magnus Fin said to Aquella in selkie thought-speak.

No. He's just concerned. Your hand was kind of strange looking.

"Religion perhaps – not my business – just – wondered? And – serious issue – truant. Always – the beach, I hear."

Fortunately Magnus Fin's mother had some acting skills. Mr Sargent had been droning on with Barbara saying little, when suddenly she jumped up, threw her hands to her face and declared, "Oh, heavens! Is that the time? Goodness! I'll miss the appointment."

"Appointment? What appointment?" Mr Sargent stumbled to his feet. The get-well cards fell from his lap and scattered onto the floor. "Oh! These are for your son."

"I'm terribly sorry, Mr Sargent. Thank you so much for coming round. I'll give these children a good telling off, and you can be sure they won't miss school again. Oh, and don't worry about my son's health. He's the healthiest boy I know. Now, oh dear, I can't believe the time. So, if you don't mind..." Barbara opened the door to usher him out. Fin and Aquella hurried up the stairs and stumbled into Fin's room. "Goodbye, Mr Sargent."

She closed the front door, leant back against it, and took a deep breath. Outside, the tyres of Mr Sargent's big car crunched down the gravel track.

"Magnus!" Barbara shouted. "Come down here!"

Magnus Fin went downstairs and stood sheepishly by the living-room door. His mother marched forward and picked up his hands. "What was he talking about?"

Fin pulled his hands back, and shrugged. "It was just a scratch from something on the beach. But it's better, honestly, it's much better."

Barbara slumped down onto the sofa and dropped her head into her hands. "Oh, Magnus," she sighed, "I'm scared for what might happen to us. You running off like that. I've told you before – it draws attention to us. Promise me you'll go to school, act like a normal boy, and stop messing about with stuff on the beach. Will you?" She turned to look at him, a pleading expression in her eyes. "Please?"

First Tarkin telling him to act normal and now his mother! Fin twisted his hair round his finger. Right then, he would. He would be so normal they wouldn't recognise him. If that was what it took to guard the selkie secret he'd do anything. But he didn't tell lies. A promise, he knew, was a promise. He couldn't promise to stop beachcombing.

"I'll go to school," he agreed, "and I'll act normal – I promise. And, Mum, don't worry about my hand. Aquella said I've got sensitive skin. It was just a scrape. I'm perfectly fine."

"That's good." She seemed relieved. "And I'm glad you're fine." She pointed to the cards scattered all over the floor. "They're for you. The teacher might think you're a bit odd, but I'd say you have lots of friends."

Fin gazed down at the cards. There were blue ones, tartan ones, big ones, multi-coloured ones. One had a drawing of a crab on it. There was even one in the shape of a whale. He felt a warm fuzzy feeling spread through his body. He bent down and scooped up the cards. He did have friends. Lots of them.

And in his Neptune's Cave of a bedroom, in the cottage down by the sea, in the far north of Scotland, Magnus Fin took down his poster of a great white shark and in its place pinned up all 22 cards.

Chapter 9

Meanwhile in southern England, on a housing estate far from the North Sea, lived Billy Mole. His bedroom was lined wall to wall with pictures of celebrities.

Billy Mole was seventeen, but told people he was "going on twenty". He had three failed careers behind him: lead singer in a Take That tribute band, shelf stacker in a large supermarket and pet sitter. None of the careers had suited him. So mostly he stayed in bed.

Out of a sense of desperation Mr Mole found his teenage son a job – a real cracker of a job with great prospects. Mr Mole knew someone who knew someone. That was how these favours worked. And this someone knew someone who owned a magazine – not the best magazine in the world, but nonetheless, a magazine. *Inside Lives* it was called. Billy Mole was going to be a junior journalist. The Mole's had great hopes for their only child.

"But I don't even know how to spell right, Dad," Billy protested the day his dad broke the news about his new job. Billy was at the fridge, downing a whole bottle of Coke.

"No prob, son," beamed Mr Mole. "They got them spell checks, ain't they? You don't need to spell right." Mr Mole winked and nudged his son in the ribs. "Think of all them celebs you'll meet. Think of all them fancy parties. You're made, son. Nuffin to it. Just snoop after footballers' wives and royalty, snap a few photos, and wham! We're rich!"

Billy was beginning to like the idea. His dad was right – who needed to spell?

"I'll need new clothes." Billy knew how to make the most of his dad's good moods.

"Anything you want, son. Just say the word. Anything at all. You'll have to get rid of that white tracksuit. Study them magazines, son. See what them celebs are wearing, then copy them." Mr Mole put his big tattooed arm around his son's shoulders and gazed about the kitchen, as though imagining it all gleaming new. Lowering his voice he said, "Don't forget us, son."

Billy shook his head, and burped. "Course not, Dad."

Mr Mole stood by the breakfast bar, staring at his son in admiration. Billy threw the empty Coke bottle into the bin. Then he fiddled with his phone. "So, the gear, Dad. I'll need a stack of notes. A stack." He continued fiddling with his phone, waiting for his dad to come up with the money.

Mr Mole frowned and eventually pulled a crisp fifty-pound note from his back pocket. "She's a beauty," he said, handing it over slowly, studying the Queen's head as he did.

Billy had hoped for more. Lots more. But he knew enough to know that fifty quid was – in the old-fashioned world of his Dad – loads. He took it, said thanks, fiddled some more with his phone, then went off to find his mum. He managed to wheedle another fifty quid from her, then, with a hundred pounds in his tracksuit pocket, he took the bus all the way into Oxford

Street in central London. Billy Mole was going to kit himself out for the big, bright, rich and famous world of journalism. He snapped his fingers. He whistled. He was going to hit the big time. Billy Mole couldn't wait!

It was dawn when a black seal lifted his head from the slack water. The seal called out – a long low call – but no one heard. Then he made for the shore, where, using his strong front flippers, he bounced, rocked and hauled up the stony beach.

A pale rose tinted the eastern horizon. The seal lay on the beach, looking like a smooth dark boulder, until he lifted his head and sniffed the cool air. Then he began to roll from side to side, popping fat seaweed pods beneath him.

As the seal rolled, he uttered a low sound, which grew louder as his movements became more vigorous – until the sound was no more the howling of an animal but of a boy singing. That wasn't the only change. The dark folds of his seal skin fell away. The skin around his flippers peeled back and in their place human hands appeared, with long human fingers. The tail fins of the seal fell back and in their place emerged legs and feet. By this time a whole seal skin lay on the beach, and from it the figure of a boy rose unsteadily to his feet.

The seal-boy scooped up fronds of seaweed and wrapped them around his body. He bent to secure his seal skin under a stone then stood upright and took a few hesitant steps across the beach. He slipped, fell over, laughed, and shakily rose to his feet again. He walked like a boy, free from crutches, who quickly masters the art of walking. Confident now, he lifted his arms high into the air then broke into a waddling run. He jumped over stones. He picked up a plastic bottle and threw it into the air. He hopped on one foot. He kicked his ankles together, and all the time he made whooping sounds, as though being a boy was the best thing in the world.

Only his strange outfit set him apart from any other teenage boy. He had slim, long limbs, a tall slim body, a face filled with enthusiasm and curiosity, bright green eyes and a fine sweep of black hair. But always as he ran, and jumped, and played, he kept a wary eye on his seal skin. Often he turned his head with a jerk, as though afraid of being discovered. And sometimes, tripping over the twisted body of a seagull or a pile of litter, he stopped, gazed downwards and sighed.

Then he ran up to the beach path, squatted down and looked along it, as though waiting for someone. Selkies, unlike humans, don't have watches. For Ronan the seal-boy, morning had long since begun. The sky was streaked with red and soon the sun would be up. He didn't dare stay on the beach long, but long enough, he hoped, to see his cousin, Magnus Fin, or his younger sister Aquella. Ronan knew enough about Magnus Fin to know he would be at the beach in the early morning hunting for finds washed ashore by the tide. After the recent storm, much had been flung from the angry mouth of the sea. Ronan plugged his nose. There was a stench of rotting fish that even for a selkie was terrible.

Ronan was desperate to see Magnus Fin and Aquella. He had news for them – good and bad. The sea hardly felt safe any more. Either it was a churning whirlpool or a stagnant grave. Magnus Fin had helped the selkies before. Ronan had taken it upon himself to ask for his help again. And, of course, there was the good news. He was bursting with it.

But where were Fin and Aquella? The fact that it was six o'clock in the morning, and both Magnus Fin and Aquella were sound asleep in their beds, meant nothing to a selkie. Many times, from the safety of the sea, Ronan had lifted his seal's head from the water and watched the little cottage on the shore, hoping to see Magnus Fin and Aquella. And sometimes he did see Aquella at the window, or Magnus Fin kicking a ball in the garden. Now here he was, on the land. Ronan had risked taking off his seal skin. It was morning, wasn't it? So where were they?

Ronan ventured along the beach, sometimes ducking behind stones in case anyone might spot him. But there was still no sign of them. Ronan was growing impatient. He couldn't risk straying far from his seal coat. And he'd never risk going up to the house. That was too close to the village. Too close to humans.

By this time the sun had well and truly risen. Ronan heard a barking noise. He glanced along the coast and could make out, in the distance, a woman with a dog. In her hand she held a long sharp stick, and she was heading his way. He had to go. He ran across the beach, found his seal skin and lay down. Like a boy slipping into a warm bathrobe, Ronan slipped into his seal skin. Down on his belly now, using his flippers to haul forward, he bounced and slithered over the stones, nosed silently into the flat sea, flicked back his tail fins and vanished under the water.

His news would have to wait.

Chapter 10

When Magnus Fin woke that Tuesday morning the first thing he did was look at his hand. What a relief. He wanted to laugh out loud. He wanted to cheer. His hand was normal! He stretched and wiggled his fingers, then bounded out of bed. He couldn't wait to go to school. He couldn't wait to see his 22 pals. He'd be as normal as...

He couldn't think. Everyone in his class was different in their own way. He pictured Robbie Cairns, who sat at the front, always handed his homework in on time and always answered questions correctly. Maybe he was normal? Fin decided Robbie Cairns was probably the most normal boy in the class, so he would model himself on him.

Robbie was a good reader. Fin rummaged in his rucksack, pulled out his reading book, bounced back on his boat-like bed, and tried to remember where he had got to. One of the pages was bent back. Probably there, he reckoned. So he read, slowly, stumbling over big words like "considered" and "mercifully". It was a story about a boy who had to pull a sword out of a stone, but then he went blind. Fin liked it, and decided he must read more often. After two pages he stopped, marked his place and put the book back, then jumped up and brushed his hair. Robbie Cairns always had well-brushed hair.

Fin decided he wouldn't go beachcombing today. Normal boys didn't do things like that – at least not before going to school. Robbie Cairns didn't. And anyway, he had plenty, didn't he? He looked around admiringly at his treasures. Bits of driftwood he'd made into mobiles swung slowly. On a shelf sat his whole collection of shells, fossils and bones. On another shelf he had arranged his special treasures, like the rusty ship's bell, the anchor, the broken plates, painted horseshoe and chipped silver saucer. And then there was the box under his bed with the really special treasures – the ones only Tarkin, and occasionally Granny May, got to see. In that secret box Fin stored his signs from the *Titanic*. GENTLEMEN, said one. DINING ROOM, said another, and his favourite – CAPTAIN'S QUARTERS. Fin loved his signs.

Of course, finding something worth a lot of money, now that would come in handy – like pirates' treasure, booty of gold and rubies hidden away in a locked treasure chest at the bottom of the sea. Or – Fin let himself think of it for a second – buried under the sand?

He tugged at his hair with the brush and tried to bat the thought away. He had decided not to think about the box thing under the sand. It spelt trouble, and who needed trouble? He felt the hairs bristle on the back of his neck. But what if... what if it really was a rusty old treasure chest?

"Magnus, Aquella – breakfast!" A delicious smell wafted up from the kitchen. His mother called again, her voice bright and cheery. "Come on, kids! I've got a treat for us – sausages!"

Fin loved sausages. He tried to forget plans to race to the beach, uncover the buried treasure (with protective gloves on this time) and make his family rich so they could have holidays and sausages every day – not only on special occasions...

Oh dear, was this a special occasion? He let the hairbrush fall to the floor. It was, and he had completely forgotten!

Quick as lightning he ripped a piece of paper from his jotter, bent it in two, fished out a blue felt pen and drew a seal. Then he drew a few crinkly waves and above that a blue sun, then inside he wrote:

Happy birthday dear Mum.
Love you loads
Magnus Fin
Xxxxx

"Good to see you here on time, Magnus Fin," said Mr Sargent, who hadn't even begun to mark the register. "And glad to see that hand of yours has gone back to normal."

Fin gave his teacher a broad smile and sat down at his desk. He thought he'd better say something (Robbie was good at conversation) so he blurted out, "It's my mum's birthday today. We had sausages for breakfast."

Mr Sargent nodded. "Me too, with scrambled eggs and black pudding. Always do." He looked again at Magnus Fin. "Hair's very smart this morning," he remarked.

Fin grinned and pulled out his reading book, at which Mr Sargent nodded again approvingly.

Maybe, thought Mr Sargent as he studied this neatly turned-out, happy looking boy, he'd got the whole thing wrong about Magnus Fin? Maybe he was just like everyone else? Maybe he really was normal? Mr Sargent pulled out the register then swept his gaze around the room. He coughed loudly to get everyone's attention. "Right then – Saul?"

"Here."

"Robbie?"

"Here."

"Tarkin?"

Silence. Everyone turned to look at Tarkin's desk.

"Where is Tarkin? Can you, by any chance, tell me, Magnus Fin?"

Fin shook his head. He swallowed hard. "No," he replied in a small voice, "I've no idea." Which wasn't quite true. He chewed the end of his ragged nail and glanced back expectantly at the classroom door. He had a very good idea where Tarkin might be. He shot a glance at Aquella.

Mermaid, she said in the selkie thought-speak, and winked.

I can't believe it, said Fin. *He was the one who said we had to act normal. Now he's running after a mermaid!*

Let's hope the beach doesn't explode, Aquella added.

Meanwhile Mr Sargent had moved on. The register was folded away. "*Ceud mile fàilte,*" he said, loudly and slowly, with a sing-song lilt to his voice.

"*Ceud mile fàilte,*" the pupils replied in their best Gaelic.

"*Ciamar a tha sibh?*" he asked, enquiring how they were.

"*Tha gu math, tapadh leibh,*" they replied in sing-song unison, saying they were doing fine, thanking you.

Magnus Fin fingered his moon-stone, hoping as he did so that his best friend Tarkin, no doubt down at the seaside mermaid hunting, was also *tha gu math*!

Chapter 11

Way down in the south of England, Billy Mole was
feeling very *tha gu math* indeed, except of course, he
didn't use those words. "Ace", that's what Billy Mole
said. He had just purchased his first suit, along with a
white shirt, black tie and black shoes. The whole outfit
cost him £62 from T.A. Mars, but was almost identical
to the one Brad Price wore in *Hi!* magazine. And that,
definitely, cost a lot more than £62!

"Very smart," the assistant commented, wrapping the
clothes up with care. "Now if my boy would only wear
something sensible like this, I'd have a lot less bother
with him."

Billy nodded, not sure what she meant. He was out
of the shop, into the nearest café, into the toilet and into
his new clothes in five minutes flat. He stuffed his white
nylon tracksuit into the plastic bag and strutted out like
he owned the place.

"Hey, you!" the waiter called. "Boy, you've got to buy
something."

But Billy was gone, striding up the street, soles
snapping – though not feeling too happy about the
"boy" bit. Didn't he look like a man, and a man with a
good job, now he owned a suit? Billy turned to examine
himself in a shop window. He hardly recognised the
stylish grown-up man that looked back. He felt great,

like he was stepping forth into the life of a celebrity journalist. *Bring it on!* That's what Billy Mole thought.

That same day, Tarkin, who had hardly slept a wink, didn't eat breakfast and couldn't face school. He wanted to tell his mum all about his mermaid, but somehow guessed she wouldn't understand. Frank, his mum's boyfriend, would probably listen to him, nodding in all the right places, but this was way too special to share with Frank.

Tarkin had first spotted his mermaid on a fishing trip in Canada with his dad. That had been three long years ago. He'd only seen her for a moment. Her beautiful head and shoulders had risen from the cold lake. With her lovely face, framed with tumbling black hair, she had gazed at him, smiled then sunk back under the water never to be forgotten. And now – on the other side of the world – she had found him. Like Tarkin always knew she would.

"Honey, you're not sick, are you? You don't look too good. Let me fetch you a vitamin C." Martha leant over the kitchen table and studied her son, chewing her lip the way she did when she was worried.

"I'm good, Mom," Tarkin said, swallowing hard. He couldn't even begin to tell his mum about bombs under the sand, swollen hands, paparazzi and mermaids. "Really, everything's cool." He took a sip of milk.

Tarkin's mum didn't look convinced. "What d'ya think, Frank? Dontcha think he's sickening for something?"

"Growing pains," suggested Frank, nodding wisely. He set down his coffee cup. "Why, now I remember when I was a boy..."

Tarkin didn't listen to what Frank remembered. Tarkin had already decided he would go to the beach. But he had to take something with him, some kind of gift. His mind raced. Jewellery – that's what mermaids like, or at least he recalled reading something like that. Tarkin fiddled with his shark's tooth necklace. No, she wouldn't want that. Mermaids are probably afraid of sharks. She needed something more – feminine. His mother cleared the dishes from the kitchen table. Frank was still going on about his boyhood.

Tarkin's mother had a jewellery box in her bedroom. Most of what was in there she'd never miss. Tarkin slunk off, muttering something about brushing his teeth. From the hallway he heard his mother clattering with pots and pans.

With the coast clear Tarkin slipped into his mum's bedroom. And there it was, right in front of him, the purple jewellery box. It sat on his mother's dressing table and seemed to beckon him. "Come to me," that's what it was saying. Tarkin had to act fast.

He tiptoed over to it and flipped open the purple, shiny lid. A necklace of pearls stared up at him – round, white, gleaming pearls. Imitation, he was sure. "Take me," they said. Tarkin stretched out his hand, his heart racing. His mother would never notice they were gone. He'd never seen her wear them. She probably didn't even like them. In a flash they were in his pocket.

"You sure you're OK, honey?"

Tarkin swung round. His mother was at the door. Had she seen him?

"Yeah, just..." He had to think quick, "looking for my scarf. It's kinda windy outside. I don't know where I left it."

"I ain't seen it," she said, walking over to her dressing table. Tarkin's heart thumped. "But here, honey." She pulled open a drawer just inches from the jewellery box. "Take one of Frank's. He won't mind."

"Thanks," said Tarkin, grabbing it and making a dash for the door. "Gotta run, don't want to be late."

And run he did – but not to school. He ran all the way through the village, over the bridge and along to the beach, with Frank's yellow scarf flapping round his neck, and his mother's pearls jingling in his pocket.

Chapter 12

When the bell rang for playtime Magnus Fin had a sore head. He had spent the Gaelic lesson, then the reading time, then the maths lesson, being as normal as he could. It was hard work looking interested all the time. Now, with the bell clanging loudly and children making a dash for the playground, he needed fresh air. He needed to slip away from the beady eyes of Mr Sargent. And he needed to find out what was up with Tarkin, who still hadn't appeared.

Children were spilling out of school, unwrapping nut bars or biting into rosy apples. Ellie and Iona begged Aquella to play skipping with them. Fin sped off across the playground.

"Hey! Where are you going?" Jake shouted after him. "We need you in goal."

Fin shook his head. He didn't like being goalie. Anyway, he needed to find Tarkin. "Playing hide and seek," Fin shouted, which was kind of true. He jumped over the wall, then as fast as he could, raced down the road that wound to the beach. Normally it took him seven minutes. If he ran super-fast he could do it in five. He practically flew down.

In no time he was pounding the sandy track he knew so well. He scanned the bay and the beach. His eyes went to his rock, the high black one that jutted out to sea. He saw a figure, hunched down on the edge of it. It was Tarkin. Fin's heart missed a beat. The water was deep there. And Tarkin couldn't swim. No matter how many swimming lessons Fin had given him, Tarkin still hadn't got the hang of it.

"Stop!" Fin yelled at the top of his voice. "Don't jump!"

But Tarkin ignored him. He was leaning so far over he would surely fall in.

In seconds Fin had reached the skerries. He leapt over the rocks. Tarkin hadn't moved. Maybe he hadn't heard him? Fin was close to him now. Trying to keep his voice calm he said, "Whatever you do, don't jump!"

Tarkin jerked his head up and cried out in fright. As he did so, the pearl necklace that he had been swinging back and forth, slipped from his fingers and fell into the sea.

"What are you doing, Tarkin?" Now Fin was by his side. "You're not a selkie. You can't go through the door. I mean, sorry but you can't even swim."

But Tarkin could only stare down into the water. "You made me drop them."

"Drop what?"

"I wanted to attract her attention. I wanted to give her a present. Oh man, I can't believe it. They've gone."

Magnus Fin glanced at Tarkin's watch. They had to get back. "What's gone? Tell me!"

Tarkin hung his head. "The pearl necklace. It was a present for the mermaid. I wanted to give her something special."

Fin stood up, hoping Tarkin would too. "She'll find them, Tark. They're in the water now, and she lives in the water. She'll get them. Don't worry. Look, we'd better get to school. It was you who said we had to act normal – now look at you! I've been so normal all morning my head hurts."

But normal seemed the last thing on Tarkin's mind. "You really think she'll find them?" he asked, still gazing into the water.

Fin shrugged. "She might. Look, come on Tark. We've got ten minutes. I'm in the good books and I want to stay there. We made a pact, remember? Mission Act Normal? We've got a secret to guard."

But Tarkin seemed unable to move. He couldn't pull his eyes away from the very place the pearls had fallen into the water.

Fin knew what was coming.

"See if you can find them, Fin. Please?"

It would waste precious time to argue, and there was something about Tarkin's pleading expression that made Fin agree. In a flash he pulled off his school clothes then, wearing nothing but his boxer shorts, he dived into the sea.

He was struck by how still everything was under the water. Even the long fronds of sea grass hung motionless. He cast his eyes around. Something glinted. He was in luck. He reached forward to pluck the pearls – only they weren't pearls but the round staring eyes of a small fish. The indignant fish darted away. Fin pulled back strands of seaweed and probed down amongst bright yellow sponges. He tugged at dead men's fingers and ran his hands over the sand. Crabs scuttled out from under dark stones. Fish circled him. Magnus Fin stretched his arms along slimy ledges and barnacled crevices near the rock. He twisted and turned, eagerly searching for anything pearl-like. Though he swept his arms through the water, no bubbles rose up. Something was not right. There was no tide, no current. In such conditions the pearls should be lying where they fell – in the sand, under the lip of rock. But they weren't. Search as he might, they weren't there. So maybe Tarkin was right? Maybe his mermaid had taken them?

Barely two minutes had passed when Magnus Fin hoisted himself up onto the rock and shook himself dry. Tarkin gave him Frank's yellow scarf to rub his hair with. "Sorry, Tark – no pearl necklace. I looked everywhere."

"So she got my present then?" His voice brightened. "She got the necklace?"

Fin pulled on his trousers, stuffed his socks into his pockets then stuck his feet into his shoes. "Yeah, I think she got it."

They were halfway up the road when the bell started to ring. Running uphill was a lot harder than running downhill. By the time they reached the wall that skirted the playground the bell sounded its last note. They leapt over the stone wall, raced across the playground and made it into the classroom in the nick of time.

"You are late, Tarkin," said Mr Sargent, pointing to the clock on the classroom wall. "Two hours to be precise. What's your excuse?"

"I had to give something to someone – honest, sir – I can't say too much about it, but believe me, it was extremely important. And if you don't mind, sir, it's personal. I'd rather not speak about it if that's alright with you."

70

There was something about the way Tarkin put his hand to his heart, said sir and spoke so earnestly that caused Mr Sargent to say nothing more on the matter. Sometimes he couldn't understand these children at all. And sometimes, it was better to believe them – even if what they said sounded mighty unusual. So he took a deep breath, nodded, then asked his American pupil – in Gaelic – "*Ciamar a tha sibh?*"

And the boy with the long blond hair, the shark's tooth necklace, two silver earrings in one ear and a damp yellow scarf looped around his neck, answered in his American accent with a Scottish twang, "*Tha gu math, tapadh leibh!*"

It was later that evening that Mr Sargent, in a local restaurant with some of his golfing buddies, after a sherry too many, mentioned his unusual pupils. Some of the golfing friends had brought along other friends who were up on holiday and Mr Sargent was in a talkative mood. The visitors listened wide-eyed to the teacher, and when they travelled home to the south they told other friends, who told others. And so it was – in the way of Chinese whispers – that in a remote village in the far north of Scotland there were some very strange children. In fact, so the rumour developed, these children probably came from another planet. Not only did one of them have two different coloured eyes, but he was probably an alien spy. And what's more, this alien seemed to possess extraordinary powers. He could, for instance, hold his breath under water for an hour! He had, so the story went, a hand the size of a house. And if doctors got hold of him they would certainly confirm he was an alien. But this alien, so the rumour went, wouldn't let doctors near him! He'd sooner die than be examined by a doctor!

The news spread like wildfire.

To be fair to Mr Sargent, he hadn't actually used the word "alien". Nor had he used the words, "fish boy". Nor had he said the hand was the size of a house. But what begins as idle chat can grow – and grow – and grow...

Chapter 13

The office of *Inside Lives* wasn't as swanky as Billy had imagined. For one, it wasn't even in London. It was in a dingy looking old warehouse on the outskirts of Milton Keynes – miles away! And the three other members of staff were dressed in dirty old jeans and baggy shirts stained with coffee and tomato sauce.

Billy swaggered into the office on day one wearing his new black suit, white shirt and black tie. His eyes roamed the poky over-heated office. No pretty girls then. In fact, no girls at all. A very large man, with his feet on the desk and a bacon roll in his hand, wolf whistled. "You'll be the new tea boy then."

Billy's heart sank even further. His dad had said journalist. He'd never mentioned tea boy. Billy looked around, wondering where his desk was. He needed to put things straight, right away. "Uh, no, Billy Mole, junior journalist," he replied, trying to sound confident, feeling a fool all dressed up in a suit.

The man sitting at the one other desk, also with his feet on it, also with bacon roll in hand, laughed. He bit into his roll and chewed noisily. "Gaza's the name."

"Hey, Gaza," muttered Billy.

The only person who appeared to be working was a younger man, maybe he was twenty, who was scrolling through emails. He was squashed at the end of Gaza's desk. "Hey, listen to this," he said, not acknowledging the new "tea boy". He peered closer to the screen. "I think my grandmother is trying to poison me. I'm sure of it. She's got strange herbs and cupboards she won't let me look into. I don't know if I should go to the police or not. Dear Hank – what do you suggest? Please help, I'm frightened for my life."

Hank, who was really called Simon, pressed delete and swung round on his swivel chair. "See, tea boy. We're supposed to print that garbage. Welcome to *Inside Lives*."

"Right. Yeah. So, where do I sit?" Billy asked, still determined to be a junior journalist. They must have got the tea boy thing wrong. He looked around for a chair and found one. He didn't know where to put the chair, so he pulled it over to a window ledge. That would do as a desk. The ledge was full of teacups. Dirty teacups.

"Good start, Billy Mole," said the big man. "I see you've found the tea department. Three sugars for yours truly, two for baldy over there, and one for Swanky Hank."

This was worse than stacking shelves. Billy bit his lip. He recalled his dad's advice that morning. "When you've not got a college degree, son, you start at the bottom and work your way up – but," he'd added quickly, "you'll be at the top before you know it." Billy picked up three cups, went to the filthy sink, and washed them.

When he'd made the tea and handed them out the big man nodded approvingly. "Make one for yourself, Billy boy. You're one of the gang now. Who knows, we might let you write a bit of gossip soon!" Simon laughed and spilt his tea. Gaza raised his eyebrows while the big man slurped loudly.

"Yeah, Billy boy," the big man went on, "you'll be at every celebrity bash in London in no time." And the three men roared with laughter.

After the first day Billy discarded the tie. He'd seen how the other men smirked. They'd said nothing but he knew what those looks meant. After the second day Billy rolled the sleeves of his jacket up, and after the third day he got rid of the trousers and wore jeans like the other men.

"Smart," said Gaza, looking him up and down. "Bit of casual, bit of neat. Very smart, Billy boy."

But they didn't like the new boy. "The young one's keen," Gaza sniffed.

"Yeah." Simon raised his eyebrows. "Too bloomin' keen."

While the big man, Simon and Gaza drank cup after cup of tea and ate bacon rolls, Midget Gems and marshmallows, doing as little work as possible, Billy was on the trail of celebrities. He devoured gossip columns. He read up on the secret lives of the stars. Any scrap of gossip concerning anyone remotely famous he exaggerated and turned into a story.

So when the phone call came, from someone who knew someone who knew someone who knew someone in Scotland, the big man looked at Gaza and Gaza looked at Simon and they all looked at Billy Mole. "Want a really big scoop?" the big man said.

Billy looked up from his window ledge. "Sure," he said, "what is it?"

The big man actually swung his legs off the table and stood up. Billy looked up at him. "Scotland, Billy boy," the big man answered. "Know where that is?"

Billy nodded, though the truth was, he wasn't sure. North, he thought. Up in the mountains – and cold. Billy wasn't liking the sound of this.

"We need you, Billy boy, in the wild and remote north of that very country."

Billy liked the sound of it even less.

"Go after this one, play your cards right and you'll be rolling in it," the boss went on. "Seems they've got an alien up there. A half-human, fish creature – looks like a boy. First of his kind. Get the story, Billy, and Vegas here you come." The big man rubbed his fingers and thumbs together. "Bit of detective work. Sounds right up your alley. Just keep a low profile, take the camera, get the evidence, then scoop an exclusive interview. We'll let you go for a week. Don't blow it, Billy boy. This could be your lucky break."

Simon and Gaza nodded. They'd be glad to see the back of him, keen as mustard and making them look like sloths. Sending him on a goose chase after an alien in the wilds of Scotland was a great idea.

"Right. Ace, boss, sounds – ace. When do I go?"

"Five o'clock tomorrow morning, Billy boy. Pack a bag. Gaza here will book you a train. You leave King's Cross and go to Edinburgh. Then change and go from Edinburgh to Inverness. Then change and go from Inverness to Wick. Then take a bus from Wick to North Point. Takes fifteen hours. Probably more with the changes. Think you can manage that?"

Billy hated the way they talked down to him, as if he was six or something. He balled his fists and deepened his voice. "Course I can."

"Been away from Mummy and Daddy before?" Simon asked in a whining voice.

Well, Billy hadn't, but no way was he going to admit that. "Course," he said, annoyed. "I'm twenty. Nearly. What do you take me for? A snot-nosed kid?"

Simon and Gaza exchanged glances and sniggered. That's exactly what they took him for.

"Good," said the big man, slumping back into his seat and swinging his legs onto the desk. "That's sorted then. Billy Mole goes to the wilds of Scotland in search of the alien."

Simon whistled and Gaza laughed out loud.

Billy gulped. Fifteen hours? He'd never been north of Watford before. He might as well be going to the moon. "Um, boss?"

The big man glanced over his shoulder. "What now?"

"Just wondering. Like, do they speak English?"

Gaza and Simon roared with laughter. The big man joined in. "Sort of," he snorted. By this time the office of *Inside Lives* was echoing with belches, sneers and side-splitting laughter.

Only Billy Mole wasn't laughing.

Chapter 14

Someone, somewhere was singing. Magnus Fin, walking home from school, stopped on the bridge and looked about him. He'd been trying hard to be normal for a few days now, but something told him all that was about to change. It was something to do with the song. It wove around him – lilting, almost dream-like – but with no singer in sight. It wasn't the wind singing. It wasn't the river. It was a woman's voice, but where was she? Was she, he leant over the bridge and peered down, in the river? As mysteriously as it had begun, the singing died away. Magnus Fin hurried across the bridge, thinking maybe he'd imagined it. Maybe the effort of trying to be Robbie Cairns was taking its toll.

But he hadn't imagined it. The song started up again. It was beautiful, mournful, and seemed to be calling him. Fin looked over his shoulder. He couldn't see anyone. He felt uneasy and was ready to run up the track when a voice broke into his thoughts:

It's me. Don't be worried, Magnus Fin! I need to speak with you.

It was Miranda's voice, but where was she? Then Fin heard a soft shuffling sound. He swung round, and gasped. Miranda stepped out from behind a crumbled stone wall near the bridge. He couldn't believe she would come this close to humans. He approached her, his heart racing. Something was wrong. What was it?

She stood on the grass in her bare feet, her long white hair cascading down her back like a waterfall. She wore a dress of red and green seaweed. Around her ankles and wrists she wore bangles of shells, but some of the shells, Fin noticed, were broken. She stretched her arms towards him.

I have checked. The coast is clear. Come over here, Fin.

Fin dropped his rucksack and hugged her. It was always thrilling to see his magical grandmother. But it was surely a serious matter that brought the selkie queen so close to humans.

"What's the matter?" he blurted out. "I mean, it's great to see you, but why did you come? Are the selkies OK?"

"It is as I feared, only worse." She took his hands in hers. "That was no mortal cut to your hand – perhaps you guessed that?"

Fin glanced at his hand. It was fine – normal – but in his mind's eye he could still see the dark thick seal skin bursting through between his thumb and forefinger. He held his breath. What would Miranda say next?

But for a moment, standing there by the stone wall, Miranda said nothing. She took a step backwards, as if trying to merge with the green moss of the old wall. Fin shot a glance along the track. Someone could appear at any second, and what would they think, seeing Magnus Fin talking to a woman with shells around her ankles and a dress of green and red seaweed?

"We have to be careful," he whispered, "someone might..."

"I know, but there are greater dangers, Fin. Listen to me. I went to see King Neptune – or I tried. The brave little crab – you know him, Neptune's most trusted servant – wouldn't let me near him. Our mighty king of the ocean is confused."

At that moment a sharp whistling sound cut through the stillness, then footsteps. Miranda pressed herself even further into the shadow of the wall. Fin peered along the track. Someone was heading their way. Frantically he looked for a better hiding place.

"Under the bridge, Miranda – quick!" Fin scooped up a stone and threw it up the hillside, hoping to distract the stranger who was heading towards them. "Run!" he hissed.

They dashed from the wall, scrambled down the bank and in seconds were hidden under the arched stone bridge. Miranda knelt down, her head bent, her arms wrapped around her chest. She looked like a beautiful statue – so still.

Usually in human form selkies use human speech, but now, with the snapping footsteps and shrill whistling of a stranger close by they switched to thought-speak.

I came here because I needed to find you quickly. It's urgent. Neptune is struggling to do his work. Too long now he has toiled without the guidance of the precious Seudan of wisdom. Perhaps Ragnor has spoken of them to you – the ocean jewels. Without them the great balance of the sea is under threat. Our dear king suffers. He will not be able to rule much longer unless his rightful treasure is returned to him.

Fin's heart leapt at the word – treasure!

Miranda went on, her thoughts swift as light streaming into his mind: *The false king stole this treasure. So much he stole. So much destruction. So much greed.*

At the mention of the false king, who Fin had defeated last summer, Magnus Fin felt his skin creep.

But Neptune's stolen treasure is not treasure as humans think of it. The Seudan are jewels from the deepest sea that bear the ancient sea-script. This script is made of secret symbols to guide the ruler of our watery kingdom. The symbols, inscribed on the jewels, instruct on the turning of the tides, the making of the waves and many secrets of the sea. These treasures mean the life of the ocean. The terrible monster stole the jewels to add to his collection of riches.

Fin's head spun with images of the awful ruins of the false king's palace. Then he started as a shrill whistling reached his ears. The whistler, whoever he was, was close. Fin's heart pounded in his chest. *Miranda! Your seal skin! Where is it?*

It is on the beach. Oh, Fin, there is so little time, please listen well. We need you to help. King Neptune has done his best without the Seudan but his power is waning. He is growing forgetful. He must have it back. When Neptune raised the storm he succeeded in tearing the treasure chest – we call it a kist – away from the ruins of the false king's palace. I believe that's what you found on the beach. King Neptune is pleased that the Seudan is safe with you. Miranda held her grandson's hand and pressed it tight.

So, I don't understand. Why did it hurt me?

The kist needs a key, Fin. Not even Neptune can open it without the key. To make sure the false king never would gain access to these treasures Neptune sealed it with magic. Anyone who tries to open the kist will burn. Only the key – in the hands of the truly good – can open this kist. Fin, you are such a one. You can breathe under the sea and you understand the magic ways. Neptune asks for your help.

Oh, Magnus Fin, this won't be easy, but I beg you – find the key.

Fin felt a hard lump in his throat. *Where is it?*

That I do not know. When the monster stormed King Neptune's cavern, looting and wreaking destruction, so much was stolen. The key may lie amongst the ruins of the false king's palace. It won't be easy to find. But you must try. You must. Then, when you have the key, wait for a sign from me and return the Seudan to Neptune.

Memory upon awful memory piled up. It had been terrible to meet the dreaded false king, and terrible to kill him. The thought of the evil one-eyed monster made Fin feel sick. Images of that rotten palace – crumbling towers, crushed creatures, the seas running red, the monster writhing in agony – haunted him. And now Miranda was asking him to go back there?

The murk and ruins of the dead monster's palace would spell death for selkies. Of course I would go if I could. I can't. Neptune can't. The crab tells me without the Seudan our sea king is losing his wisdom and powers. The sea suffers. You have seen for yourself. But with your human strength – and your selkie soul – you can go there, Magnus Fin.

At that moment a dull noise reached them from the path just metres away. Fin recognised it as his rucksack being kicked aside. Then the snapping footsteps carried on up the track, growing distant.

Miranda, your seal skin. I don't know who that person is, but I think he's heading for the beach. You have to go.

Say you'll help, Fin. Neptune's power will not last much longer. He is the true keeper of the Seudan. They must be returned. We believe in you, Magnus Fin.

He looked at her, poised as still as stone, but under that stillness, he knew, her selkie heart was breaking.

Yes, yes, I'll help, but please, Miranda, save your seal skin. Frantically Magnus Fin peered out from under the bridge. *I can see him. It's a man – he's young – I don't know him. He's not from around here, and I think he's going to the beach.*

Go and search for the key when the sky's great lantern will guide you. You have two days to prepare yourself. Now that I've done what I came here to do, I will go. But first, fetch me a coat.

Fin sprinted up the track and into the cottage. He sped up the stairs and into his parent's bedroom, pausing for a second to glance out of the window. The young man who wore a black jacket was now walking along the beach path. Fin fumbled in the wardrobe, pulled out his mother's good red coat and ran back outside with it.

Miranda, at Fin's signal, stepped out from under the bridge. She leapt lightly up the bank and put one arm through a sleeve of the coat. "Where is it now, Fin, the kist? Where is it?"

"In the sand. Tarkin and Aquella buried it again."

Miranda pulled on the other sleeve. "It can't be left there. With Neptune's rages he might whip up another storm and it'll go – back out to the vast ocean – then the Seudan will be lost for ever. You must dig it up then cover it with kelp. Don't touch it with your hands. You have to keep it safe. Keep it in the cave." Miranda pulled the red coat tightly about her.

"And then what?" said Fin, tugging at her coat, pulling her back. "How am I going to find the key?"

Miranda bent to kiss her grandson. "I am doing all I can – believe me. But it isn't easy. The swell pulls one way, then the other. Whirlpools appear and vanish as though the sea no longer knows what to do." She hurried now along the beach path. Fin ran alongside her. "I will try to find someone to help you. We have two more days. Neptune will descend into madness if he endures another moon without the Seudan. Bless you, son of Ragnor, *Sliochan nan Ron*." And with that she quickened her pace, leaving Magnus Fin far behind. In seconds Miranda was down at the beach.

The man was close to the place where she had left her seal skin. But this man wasn't used to walking on a pebble beach. He stumbled and swore. He scuffed his shiny shoes. Twice he fell over.

He turned and stared as a woman in a red coat with long white hair and bare feet sped past him. Around her ankles shells jangled. He watched her scoop something silvery up from the sand. She pressed whatever it was to her then ran off. In the next moment she seemed to vanish into thin air.

Billy Mole scratched his head, staggered to his feet, then decided he was suffering from the effects of fifteen hours travelling and the wind. It was supposed to be summer, yet it was freezing. Shivering, he watched a silver seal slip into the water. He spied something red on the rocks. A tern dive-bombed dangerously close to his head. He yelled, and ducked. Beneath him the seaweed stunk. Dead fish ponged. Billy Mole held his nose, turned on his heels and hurried off to the warmth and comfort of his bed and breakfast.

Chapter 15

Later that evening Magnus Fin and his father Ragnor took a walk down to the beach to fetch the red coat. Fin wanted to tell his father about Neptune's lost treasure but struggled to find the words. He was far more of a selkie these days than his father, who had come ashore, married a human woman and lost his seal skin. Now Ragnor spent most of his waking hours helping out on a nearby farm. It was seldom he went fishing, seldom he sat in the old cave and made fires. But he knew something was up. The sea bit in him as strong as it ever did. It pained him to see the dead fish and dead birds washed up on the tideline. He slowed his pace as they drew near to the skerries. Ahead a red coat lay folded on the black rocks.

"So she came to see you?" Ragnor asked. The why was unsaid but hung in the air.

"Yes. Dad, you've heard of the Seudan?" Fin asked.

Ragnor nodded and slowly spoke, "The secret script of the sea, etched upon the ancient jewels, written so that the wisdom will never be forgotten – of tides, of waves, of seasons. Yes, son, I know the Seudan. When you were a bairn I told you stories of the great Seudan. Your eyes used to light up, just like Neptune's jewels. Have you forgotten?"

A distant memory rose in Fin then. The old stories round the fire, of dolphins, whales, brave seals and powerful jewels.

"Aye, you remember." Then Ragnor looked out to sea. The slack water barely moved. It seemed to teem with death not life. "It's gone – is that what Miranda told you?"

"It's not gone. It's in the cave in a locked kist."

Ragnor paled. To have the Seudan – for a selkie – is like a schoolboy keeping the crown jewels under his bed. Fin ran and scooped up his mother's coat and swung round, the bright red striking against his black hair.

"It's the key that's lost. That's what Miranda wants me to find. Then return the Seudan to Neptune."

Ragnor shook his head in amazement. "My son, to think I brought you into this strange world. I thought it would be simple. I thought I, a man from the sea, could marry a woman from the land. I thought with love anything would be possible. Believe me, son, I wanted a peaceful life for you. I wanted you to grow up strong and happy and... normal, like other boys! I'm sorry. I filled your head with the selkie stories. I poured my love of the sea into you. And now..."

"But, Dad, I'm happy to be this way. Really."

"Neptune bless you, son. It is so seldom a child of both worlds is born. You are a saviour to the selkies." He clasped Magnus Fin to him, Barbara's red coat squashed warm between them. "And you're just a young laddie."

"I'll find the key to the Seudan," Fin said, surprised at the power in his voice. The last thing in the world he wanted to do was to return to the ruins of the false king's palace, but he repeated the words, the strong arms of his father wrapped about him. "I will. I'll find it!"

The next morning in the changing room while they were getting ready for gym, Magnus Fin inched along

86

the bench to where Tarkin was struggling with his laces. "Want to give me a hand?"

"Sure," Tarkin said, then his eyes lit up and he left off fiddling with his laces. "You've seen her? You've seen my mermaid?"

"No."

Tarkin looked disappointed. "Well, what then? Like, I thought we were on Mission Act Normal?"

"We are, but..."

Tarkin grinned. He was secretly growing tired of acting so normal all the time. The prospect of a good adventure set his blood stirring. Fin was about to launch into the meeting with Miranda when Tarkin beat him to it.

"Know my mermaid, Fin?"

"Yes?"

"Well, I've been thinking."

"Uh-huh?"

"That if *she* made it, like, all the way to Scotland, maybe my dad will make it too!"

Fin didn't know what to say. It had been a few weeks now since Tarkin had received as much as a postcard from his dad. Fin knew how much he missed him.

"You never know, Tark," he said, trying to sound positive, "he might."

Tarkin tucked his long orange laces into his trainers and stood up. It was time to play basketball, so nothing more was said – about mermaids, Dads or treasure chests, but Fin could see the look in Tarkin's eyes. So it wasn't only the mermaid he was thinking about, it was his dad. Fin hoped, for Tarkin's sake, that one day his dad really would turn up, but it seemed unlikely.

It was fish for lunch that day and peas. Tarkin was the only boy in school to ask for a whole lemon to squeeze on his fish. Fin tried to fork his peas but they kept rolling away. The dining room was a din. Fin toyed with his food, waiting till most people had gone, then he leant across the table.

"You said you'd help me. So, fancy a bit of treasure digging?"

Tarkin speared a slice of tomato. "Sure. Like, what kinda treasure you got in mind?"

Fin leant even further over and whispered so loudly he practically hissed, "The thing in the sand – we need to wrap it in kelp."

Tarkin chewed his tomato then leant towards Fin. "I thought we were just gonna leave it and forget about it? Mission Act Normal is working. Sargent thinks you're the best. He thinks you are so normal. And I need to protect my mermaid. Don't want folk frightening her off." Tarkin looked over his shoulder. The dinner lady was glaring at him.

"Hurry up, laddies," she shouted, "we've not got all day to wait on you."

Fin forgot his peas. "Meet me at sunset tonight. I've got two garden spades. We can use those." Fin spotted Tarkin's reluctance. "Oh come on, Tark. It'll be fun. And I've got rubber gloves. Look, it's important. Really important." Magnus Fin put his plate on his tray and shifted in his seat, ready to stand up. "But if you don't want to help, I'll do it on my own."

Tarkin put his plate onto his tray, bit his lip then nodded. "OK, buddy. Count me in. It just freaked me out. Your hand was gross. But sure, I'll help. Just don't forget the gloves."

"I won't. I've got everything we need. I got it all ready last night."

"So if I'm gonna help do I get in on the secret? Like, what is it, this *thing* in the sand?"

Magnus Fin glanced at the ruddy-faced dinner lady who was drumming her fingers on the counter at the hatch. Fin looked sideways at Tarkin. "King Neptune's stolen treasure," he whispered, then rose and hurried off with his tray.

That afternoon in school minutes seemed like hours. Magnus Fin had forgotten all about Robbie Cairns and had fallen back into his old habit of gazing out of the window. Absent-mindedly he doodled hammerhead sharks on the cover of his jotter. He didn't put up his hand once to answer a question, and when Mr Sargent asked Magnus Fin to stand up and read a poem, he stuttered, went red, didn't know how to pronounce "chapman billies" and had no idea what "drouthy" meant.

Mr Sargent looked crestfallen. His star pupil wasn't shining now. Fin bit his nails and hung his head. "You disappoint me," was all Mr Sargent could say. "Sit down."

What are you thinking about?

Fin glanced over his shoulder. Aquella winked at him. *Cos it's certainly not "Tam O'Shanter", that's for sure!*

Fin giggled. Mr Sargent glared at him. "First you make a complete hash of our national poet," bellowed the teacher, "then you sit there and titter. Well, it's not funny. Not one bit!"

Magnus Fin tried to pull himself together. Detention was the last thing he needed on this day of all days. He stared down at his desk, but still Aquella hounded him, jabbing her thoughts into his mind.

Something's going on. What is it?

Fin's mind raced. *I've been asked to protect the thing in the sand. We're going to the beach tonight at dusk. It could be Neptune's stolen treasure. I would have told you, but your skin... You can't risk being close to the sea. The tide will be up. I didn't want to give you more to worry about.*

I knew it! I had a hunch. Something's wrong, isn't it?

I'll tell you later. Except selkie thought-speak didn't manage secrets well. Aquella had already picked up on the thought he was trying not to think: *King Neptune's dying.*

She gasped.

"Are you alright, Aquella?" Mr Sargent asked, now knitting his bushy eyebrows in her direction.

Aquella coughed and stammered, "Ye-yes. Ah, sorry – I'm fine."

Then he swung round to Tarkin who was chewing the end of his ponytail, a habit Mr Sargent deplored. "You're very quiet this afternoon, Tarkin," he remarked. "Why don't you stand up and give us all a bit of Rabbie Burns, eh?"

Reluctantly Tarkin rose to his feet, fumbling to find the right page. The book shook as he tried to make sense of the words. "When chapman – bill – um, sorry – billies – leave the street," he read, painfully slowly, "and – dru... no, um – and drouthy – neigh – um, neebours, neebours meet..."

Never had the clanging of the school bell sounded so sweet. Leaving Tam O'Shanter to stare at dancing witches, Tarkin dashed out of the classroom, followed by Magnus Fin, followed by Aquella. They didn't stop running till they reached the bridge over the river.

"OK, Tarkin," Fin gasped, dumping his rucksack on the grassy verge. "Meet me outside the house when the sun starts to set, and we'll go down to the beach and dig up the treasure. Aquella – if you want to join us – you can be on lookout."

Aquella looked horrified while Tarkin, who had now forgotten all about Magnus Fin's gross hand, looked delighted. "Man, I can't wait. What a blast! Treasure! We are gonna be so rich."

"It's not ours," Fin said, picking up his rucksack and slinging it over his back. "It's Neptune's. The false king stole it. And we can't open it because we haven't got a key." Not yet – he didn't say. He didn't want to think about trying to find the key.

Tarkin nodded. Aquella shuddered. Any mention of the false king set her reeling. He had taken her prisoner, and destroyed her seal skin. Fin saw her frown.

"Look, it's OK, Aquella. Me and Tark – we'll deal with this. We'll dig it up at dusk. You don't have to come along. We'll be fine."

"Cool," said Tarkin, "I like dusk. Dusk is when bats and owls come out. Good time for adventure. Ghosts too maybe."

"Dusk is when dog walkers stay indoors," said Fin flatly, "I hope."

"And when the moon is full," added Aquella, "dusk is when selkies haul out on good flat rocks, take off their seal skins and dance."

"Nice!" Tarkin whistled. "And what about mermaids?"

"They come out of their sea caves to splash in the shallow water wearing pearl necklaces," Fin said and laughed.

Tarkin's blue eyes widened and his jaw dropped. "Seriously?"

"Joke." He winked. "But you never know, Tark, it could be true."

Chapter 16

Dusk fell. Aquella said she felt tired so stayed indoors, while Magnus Fin and Tarkin hurried along the beach path, each carrying a garden spade and saying not a word. There was something about dusk that demanded silence. The land lay still. As Fin had hoped, no one was around. It was balmy that evening and the sea was flat. Fin wore his wetsuit. Even in early June, balmy or not, the sea would be cold.

"You stay here, Tark. I'll fetch the kelp."

And he did. He fetched up loads of it, tearing up thick fronds and wrapping it round his arms. He saw how fish moved heavily, as though dragging their silvery bodies through the sad sea. Magnus Fin plunged deep into the sea, parted thick swathes of kelp, then jolted back in shock.

Good lad. I said to Miranda, "Magnus Fin will set it all to right."

Fin gaped at the tiny pink crab that clung to a twist of sea grass.

With your mouth open like that, you resemble a dogfish. We have a little saying down here: if the tide turns you'll stay like that! And you wouldn't want that, Magnus Fin!

Fin snapped his mouth shut. The crab hopped down to land on strands that grew closer to the seabed. *Here, Magnus Fin. Take a few of these. They're the best!*

With that, the tiny crab paddled off and vanished into the dark water. Fin felt a surge of energy at meeting his old friend. He couldn't help liking the crab, even though he always seemed to volunteer him for the ocean's most dangerous quests. He had been there when Magnus Fin defeated the false king, and he had guided him towards discovering what was poisoning the selkies last autumn. And how, Fin wondered, tearing up the very fronds the crab had suggested, did something so small come to be so powerful? He was King Neptune's right-hand man.

Tarkin was guarding the patch of sand with two spades at the ready when Fin reappeared, bent under what seemed a mountain of seaweed. "Ugh!" Tarkin held his nose. "It pongs."

"But it'll protect us." Magnus Fin set the bounty of kelp down on the sand and picked up his spade. "You ready to dig?"

Tarkin pulled on the bright orange rubber gloves. "Sure thing, buddy." Then he too picked up his spade. They started to dig.

Dusk was fast turning into night. The first stars came out and the silvery moon rose while Fin and Tarkin jabbed their heavy garden spades into the damp sand. The faster Fin dug, the slower Tarkin dug, until his enthusiasm evaporated and he stopped altogether.

"Look, I dunno about this. I think we gotta act sensible."

Magnus Fin threw back another spadeful of sand then stared at his friend. "Sensible? I've been so sensible for a whole week. I was the star pupil. I've almost read a whole book. Anyway, Tark, you're the one who's always telling me to go for it – be adventurous. I thought you couldn't stand sensible?"

Tarkin looked glumly into the hole, as though imagining some infectious fiend down there. "Yeah, well, I can change my mind." The spade hung limply in his hand.

"Come on, Tark. You've seen how dead the sea looks, or else wild like it's angry. It's not right. And if you're going to be friends with me you've got to get used to stuff like this. Think about it – Neptune needs this back. Without it the sea'll be no place for any creature to live. No place for your mermaid."

At the mention of the mermaid Tarkin's enthusiasm returned. "OK," he said, lifting the spade, "when you put it that way, I'm with you. Let's dig!"

Tarkin grinned, and dug. Any doubts and fears soon turned to excitement. Simply being out on the beach under the slowly darkening sky, digging for treasure, was adventure enough. They flung up damp sand. In no time they hit metal. Fin fumbled for the torch and shone it down the hole.

"Look, Tarkin, that's it."

Tarkin peered down the hole, squinting to see. "It doesn't look much like treasure."

Fin flashed the torch around, showing up rusty bumps and studs. Tarkin was right: it didn't look like treasure at all. Maybe Miranda had got it all wrong? Fin tried to stay positive.

"Anyway, we have to dig round it then bring it up." With his dad's big garden spade he could work quickly. He sliced the damp sand, circling the thing, which wasn't as huge as he'd at first thought. "We've gone right round it," he announced, panting with the effort. "OK, Tark, I'm going to dig under it then lever it up."

But levering it up wasn't easy. The thing was heavy. Tarkin lay down his spade and joined Fin, leaning down on the wooden handle to force it upwards.

"It's coming, buddy," Tarkin shouted, forgetting about the silence of dusk. "Oh boy, oh boy – it's coming up!"

"Hold it tight, Tark. Don't wobble. We don't want it to fall back down!"

They succeeded in raising the thing a few inches, then a few more. "It's not huge," Fin yelled, "but it's kind of heavy."

"It's like one of those old boxes people used to put coal in," Tarkin yelled. "Easy does it, we've got to swing the spade up and lower it onto the sand. You ready, buddy?"

"I'm ready."

Leaning down on the handle they tilted the spade up. The thing was coming into view, though in the dusk all they could see was a dark shape. Panting, they swung the spade slowly round then lowered the metal box onto the sand.

"Right, Tark," Fin cried, "we've nearly done it. We have to slip the spade away from under it. OK, let's do it!"

They did it, leaving the box sitting in front of them.

"Shine the torch on it, Fin. Quick! Let's have a good look at this treasure chest. Oh man, what a blast!"

"It's called a kist," Fin said, groping for the torch. "That's what Miranda said." He switched it on and swung it in the air. As he did so the white glaring beam from the torch lurched round, lighting up the retreating form of a man hurrying along the beach path.

Fin and Tarkin froze. "Who's that?" they both said.

"I think it's that man I saw," Fin whispered. "That stranger."

The kist on the sand sat like a rusty secret, glinting in the torchlight. Magnus Fin and Tarkin were afraid now. Tarkin wanted to leave, but Fin wanted to stay. "We can't just leave it here. Come on, Tark. That man's gone. Whoever he was, he's not here now. And anyway we need to cover it with kelp and hide it in the cave."

Fin dragged a heap of kelp towards the rusty kist. Tarkin stared as Fin pulled out long strands of seaweed and wrapped them around the box, as though he was bandaging it.

"You can help, you know," Fin whispered. "Take some seaweed and wrap it. We have to totally cover it."

"OK. Yuk, it's kinda smelly." They spoke like spies, in hushed whispers, wrapping the kist until every inch of rusty metal was covered. Every few seconds Tarkin glanced over his shoulder.

Magnus Fin was also worried about the stranger on the beach. He was the same man he'd seen when Miranda had come ashore; he was sure of it.

"Right, we have to carry it up to the cave and hide it there. You ready?"

"It looks heavy," Tarkin whispered.

"We have to try. Come on. You go on that side, I'll go on this side. Hurry."

Tarkin looked pale in the torchlight, but though he was frightened he nodded. "OK," he whispered, squatting down beside the wet, smelly box, "let's do it! One... two..."

Sharing the weight, they staggered up the beach towards the cave. With rubber gloves on, and slimy seaweed to grapple with, the kist slipped and wobbled. It was heavy but they were strong and determined. When they reached the darkness of the cave they lowered the kelp-covered kist down to the sand.

Panting hard, Tarkin hurried to the mouth of the cave and shone the torch along the beach. There was, he reported, no sign of the stranger. "Weird," he muttered, slinking back into the cave, "seriously weird." He shone the light on to the seaweed lump. "Aren't you gonna open it?" he asked, his voice trembling with anticipation.

"No, Tark, we're going to stow it away in a dark corner, heap a bit more seaweed over it, then leave it. It needs a key. Didn't I tell you?"

"We did all that and we can't open it?"

"Not yet. Tark, that was the easy bit. And thanks for your help. I really appreciate it." Fin dropped one more clump of dried seaweed over the kist. "It'll be fine now. Even that strange man we saw snooping about would never guess there's a treasure chest under here."

Tarkin peeled off the rubber gloves and stepped back. "I think we should get out of here. It's late."

Magnus Fin stared down at the pile of seaweed. Was Neptune's treasure really hidden under that? And if he went all the way back to the ruins of the monster's palace – assuming he could find the ruins of the monster's palace – and if he found a key – and that was surely a massive if – how likely was it that the key would fit this kist?

"Come on!" urged Tarkin from the mouth of the cave. "Let's split."

The bat that slept on the high ledge where Magnus Fin kept his seal skin swooped around the cave, snapping him from his wonderings.

They hurried along the beach path to the cottage, hardly needing the torch now, for the waxing moon had risen and lit their way. Tarkin had left his bike leaning against Fin's garden wall. He swung onto the saddle and was ready to pedal away when he said in a hushed voice, "Maybe I was right about the paparazzi? Like, maybe they've really come!"

Magnus Fin pushed open the front door of the cottage, the image of the stranger in the beam of torchlight haunting him. Maybe Tarkin was right. Maybe they really had.

Chapter 17

The paparazzi was back taking notes in the Rugged Coast Bed and Breakfast. Billy Mole, pressed up against the radiator, wrote in his notebook,

In this place boys play on the beech in the dark, and it's cold.

Because it was chilly and dark and windy, Billy Mole hadn't been in any mood to hang about. "You might find these aliens down at the beach so head on down there first thing," that's what the big man had told him. The big man had not told him you might also catch your death of cold!

Shivering and tired, Billy hadn't lingered down at the beach. Was it, he wondered, the norm for Scottish boys to play on the beach at night with not an adult in sight? And was it the norm for women to run along the beach in strange costumes then vanish into thin air? And these boys he'd seen, what were they so excited about? "Treasure!" Billy had heard them shouting. They appeared to be digging. "We'll be rich!" one of them had shouted. Billy was curious. Rich was something that interested him big time. But the wind had biting teeth, and he'd felt splats of rain. Billy had made a mental note of where the boys were.

Maybe he'd come back later and have a look at that treasure himself.

Then he had turned and stumbled over the stony beach in a hurry to get back to the warmth of the Rugged Coast Bed and Breakfast. There he would hatch a plan, and try to track down this schoolteacher who said he was teaching aliens. Billy had shivered, pulled up the collar of his jacket, and scampered off.

After he had warmed up and eaten two of Mrs Anderson's bacon rolls, Billy Mole went off into the night in search of the schoolteacher. The big man said this teacher played golf and the place to find him would be in the golf club, so that's where Billy went, bending into the wind and missing home already.

The schoolteacher was easy to spot, with his handlebar moustache and his red cheeks. Billy downed his Coke and chuckled to himself; this was going to be a cinch. He'd have his sensational story in next to no time. Billy waited until the man was on his own, sitting down to a cup of coffee. Billy strutted over, feeling generous. When his story hit the headlines, there'd be money in it for this teacher.

Billy sat down next to the teacher and grinned. "It was you, wasn't it? What put me on the trail of them aliens?"

Mr Sargent spluttered. His coffee cup shook in his hand. "I'm sorry. I don't know you, and I don't know what the devil you're on about. Now – if you don't mind – I'm actually waiting for someone."

"That's me! We got your tip-off and here I am. Billy Mole – *Inside Lives* magazine. Come all the way from London and I just need to ask you a few questions, like."

Mr Sargent's face had gone redder than usual and his eyes flickered around the clubhouse. Lowering his voice he said, "Look, you've obviously mistaken me for someone else. Now, please, I must ask you to sit elsewhere."

But Billy Mole wasn't going anywhere. He waggled his notebook in the air. "Not what you was saying before. Yeah. It was you. Big old-fashioned army type. Moustache and ruddy cheeks. Plays golf. Ain't nobody else fits that bill, is there?"

Mr Sargent looked desperately around the clubhouse. Two women sat together in the corner, and a slim young man with no moustache stood at the bar. Billy went on, sounding super-confident, "Yeah, you was telling the whole world how you got aliens in your class. Well, here I am, come to get the whole story."

Mr Sargent coughed. Beads of sweat glistened above his bushy eyebrows. "Look here, laddie, I said nothing of the sort. Nothing!" But his voice had lost its usual robust vigour. He bent his head towards Billy Mole and in a pleading, almost child-like voice said, "It's all a misunderstanding. You've got the wrong end of the stick."

Billy Mole laughed. "Bit late now. This story's gonna be a sensation. It goes public next week. The man what teaches aliens! Ha! So, tell me, what are they like? Them fish folks – can they read? Have they got funny habits? Do they by any chance muck about at night-time down at the beach, digging for treasure?"

Mr Sargent squared his shoulders and whipped out his mobile phone. "Listen, sonny boy, if you don't beat it I – I'm going to call the police!"

Billy Mole wasn't too keen on the police, so he got up and he beat it, leaving Mr Sargent dabbing his brow with his handkerchief. After the flashy know-it-all teenager left the golf club Mr Sargent fumbled in his pocket for a barley sugar.

"Oh dear," he muttered, tugging off the wrapper, "oh dear, dear, dear – what on earth have I done?"

At nine o'clock the next morning, it dawned on Billy Mole that he had an informant staring him in the face. Mrs Anderson! If the schoolteacher wasn't going to come up with the goods, she surely would. He knew what old wives were like for gossip.

"Morning, laddie," she sang, setting a bowl of piping hot porridge down in front of her sole guest. "Now, eat this up. It'll put flesh on your bones."

Billy stared at the porridge and screwed up his face, but decided he'd give it a go. He needed to sweeten up the old woman, and forcing himself to eat a few spoonfuls of porridge was all in a day's work for a celebrity journalist.

"And for after," went on Mrs Anderson, "are you for black pudding or smoked kippers?"

Billy felt sick, but he kept going, kept spooning the porridge into his mouth. With five heaped spoonfuls of sugar it didn't taste too bad. He looked up at her. "So that's the secret then? Smoked kippers?"

Mrs Anderson bent her head closer. "Now, laddie, and what secret would that be?"

Billy Mole hated this laddie thing, but he smiled on. "Oh, you know, the secret of them different coloured eyes. I heard there's a shed load of them up here."

Mrs Anderson looked confused. "Sorry, laddie. I'm not following yea."

"You must've seen them. These..." Billy forced himself to say the word, "laddies... with different coloured eyes."

Mrs Anderson tossed her head back and roared with laughter. And then it fell – right into Billy Mole's lap. "You mean Ragnor and Barbara's laddie, wee Magnus Fin?"

Billy tried not to look triumphant. "Oh, yeah. Magnus Fin. Yeah. That's him. Him that's always down at the beach."

"Well, he would be, wouldn't he? He practically lives there." Mrs Anderson went over to the window, pulled back the net curtain and pointed. "Way down on the shore. See that wee stone cottage, standing all on it's own? That's where he lives." Then she smiled and let the curtain fall back. "More laddies like him and the world would be a better place. Now, was that one kipper you were for, or two?"

Billy Mole had all the information he wanted, so there was no need to be sweet with doddery old Mrs Anderson any more and suffer kippers. He pushed the porridge bowl away. "Get me a bacon roll."

"Charming!" she sniffed, clearing away his bowl. Then she hurried off to the kitchen, tutting loudly. "Charming indeed!"

Billy Mole laughed, whipped his notebook from his jacket pocket and wrote down two words:

magnis fyn

Chapter 18

That afternoon Aquella took her homework and headed down to the beach. The tide was well out and craggy rocks, usually submerged, made small islands in the sea. Aquella didn't have to worry about salt water damaging her skin when the tide was safely out. She walked along the beach path with her reading book tucked under her arm. A sea mist rolled in over the water. She liked mist. She liked how it swirled and hid things.

As she walked she sang a haunting quiet song. When she sang she could imagine rolling with the ebb and flow of the tides. She could be a seal again. She could forget how her seal skin was well and truly gone, ripped to shreds by the awful monster, the same that had stolen Neptune's treasure. The same, she thought with a deep feeling of relief, that had been killed by Magnus Fin. Aquella stopped singing and gazed out to sea, glad there were no monsters any more. Her eyes fell to the hole in the sand. She shuddered, thinking about the great task King Neptune was asking of Magnus Fin.

It was hard enough being a selkie with no seal skin. She wondered what it was like to be a boy of both worlds. The selkies considered Magnus Fin their hero, she knew that. But often when she looked at him, spooning Rice Krispies into his mouth at a great rate, or skimming stones, or collecting shells and bones from the beach, she saw simply a skinny, shy, dreamy boy. He didn't look like a hero at all. Were they expecting too much of him?

She sighed and picked up the thread of her song. She sang to the oystercatcher that was using its chisel-like orange beak to crack open a shellfish. Then she plonked herself down on a soft clump of marram grass, lay back, kicked off her shoes, and opened her book.

It was the book about the boy who had turned blind. Aquella had only been ashore for nine months, but could read as well as any eleven-year-old. And she felt very sorry for the boy. He knew people by their voices, she read, which was strange, because at that moment Aquella heard something. She lowered her book and listened. It sounded like a soft howling. She glanced along the beach. No one was there. She looked behind her, but still couldn't see anyone. The mist rolled towards her. "Haar", that's what Ragnor called it. Out of the haar the soft howl came again.

Aquella jumped to her feet. She knew that call. Deep in her selkie bones she knew that call. Her open book fell onto the sand. "Yes?" she called, peering out to sea. "Yes? Who's there?" Her voice rose with excitement. Now she was sure, the call was coming from the sea. Aquella stared. Was it the swirling mist or was that black rock in the water moving? She ran a few steps forward but didn't dare go further. "Yes?" she called again. "Who is it?"

Aquella gazed open-mouthed as a black seal emerged from the mist and slithered up onto the rock. The seal rolled itself from side to side, until the seal skin fell back and a girl stood up. The girl on the rock had long black

106

hair. It spilt down her back. She swung her head and her hair wrapped itself around her and clung to her like a dress.

"Aquella?" the girl on the rock called. "It is you, isn't it?" The girl lifted an arm and waved.

Aquella, jumping up and down with excitement, waved back. "Lorelie?" she called. "*Fàilte*, Lorelie!" Tears sprang to her eyes. Lorelie had been like a kind older sister to Aquella. It was Lorelie who had taught her the old Gaelic songs. It was Lorelie she had turned to when she felt afraid or lonely. And like Aquella, Lorelie too had been a prisoner of the false king, forced to sing whenever he snapped his tentacles. And when Aquella had lost her seal skin it had been Lorelie who had comforted her.

"Yes. It's me. It's Aquella! Oh Lorelie!" she shouted "Lorelie!"

Lorelie secured her seal skin, pressing it into a crevice in the rock. Then she dived into the sea. Seconds later she emerged, clad in a red and green dress of seaweed and a necklace of shells. She stood up in the shallow water, shook out the thick coils of her long dark hair then took a shaky step forward. Aquella watched. She knew that time well, moments after the change, when the new body feels as if it might topple over.

From the shore Aquella urged her friend on. "Take it easy, Lorelie. Don't tread on glass. Careful. That's great."

Lorelie stepped from the water and onto the pebbles. The seal-girl gazed at Aquella, clapped her hands together and laughed. Water dripped from her dress and her hair clung to her. More than anything Aquella wanted to run to her friend and hug her, but she couldn't risk getting salt water on her skin, not even a drop.

"I know," Lorelie said, stretching her arms out. "I won't wet you. I just want to see you." Then Lorelie, in that waddling selkie way, ran to Aquella, pausing just inches from her. Glistening tears sat on Lorelie's long black eyelashes. "I've missed you so much," she said, wiping her tears with her hair. "We've all missed you."

Aquella felt hot tears prick her eyes. "And I've missed you – so much. I'm a land girl now. My skin change is almost done. I miss the sea, of course I do, but it's good being human. I sing the songs you taught me. People here say I've got a good voice."

Lorelie stood as close as she dared, a graceful smile lighting her face. "Oh, Aquella. You look beautiful and different somehow. What's it like wearing human clothes?"

Aquella laughed, looking down at her jeans and thick blue fleece top. "You get used to it I suppose. Well, except shoes. They pinch. I kicked them off. I don't think I'll ever get used to them."

Their clear voices rang out over the water and through the mist. "Oh my dear Aquella, listen to me." A tone of sadness crept into Lorelie's words. "I bring good news and bad. Things have changed. Miranda has told us how King Neptune is losing his power, how the Seudan is lost. The sea is hardly safe any more. Pounding waves buffet us, then the next moment we are dragged down as though the sea is a dead weight. And when we want to come to the safety of the land Miranda forbids us. She says it is growing dangerous for selkies to remain so close to humans. She says nowhere is safe."

Just then a harsh voice cut through the mist, "Oi!" followed by the fast crunching noise of feet pounding over stones. Aquella swung round. Out of the thick mist the voice came again. "Oi! You!" Aquella couldn't see anyone. Her heart raced. The footsteps were coming closer.

"You see!" gasped Lorelie. "We must be quick. Miranda tells us Magnus Fin will find the key. She tells us he will return the Seudan. The key to Neptune's treasure, Aquella, do you remember? The great white shark boasted about how he knew where it was, back in the false king's palace."

"Lorelie, you'd better go!"

But Lorelie had already gone. Hearing a splash Aquella glanced back at the rock just in time to see two tail fins flick upwards then vanish under the water. Lorelie had left, taking her good news with her – for nothing had been good. Nothing.

Aquella left her book in the sand and ran. But selkies are not fast runners. Great swimmers, yes, but running doesn't come naturally to them. If Fin was a good runner it was because he was half human. Aquella was one hundred per cent selkie. She waddled. She took small rolling steps. She stuck her arms out to the side.

But now, with a human chasing her, she ran like never before. If she could only get as far as the cave she could hide. There were nooks and crannies there he'd never find. She didn't dare look back. Behind her footsteps crashed down over the pebbles. "Oi! You!" he kept shouting. "I want to talk to you!"

Aquella kept running, the way she'd seen Tarkin run in school sports, pumping his elbows back and forth and taking long leaping strides. She felt exhausted. The footsteps sounded louder. Any moment now he would pounce on her. This was surely the boy Magnus Fin and Tarkin had spotted, the one they called the snooping stranger. The cave was still a long way off.

"What's the panic? Hey! You! I want to talk to you!" Billy Mole was right behind her. The next second he overtook her then swung round and barred her way. "Hang on," he panted. "I want to ask – just a few – questions!"

Whimpering like a trapped animal Aquella stared up at him, terrified. But this strange boy, she sensed, seemed equally unsure of her. His eyes, she saw, had fallen to her bare feet. She tried to wriggle her webbed toes down into the sand.

"Too late," he gasped. "My God! That's not normal. You're one of them fish girls, aren't you?"

"I'm a land girl," Aquella blurted out. "I'm normal." She flashed a look out to sea. Lorelie had gone.

"Oh yeah," Billy said, "and I'm a pig flying in the air. Who you kidding? Nobody goes round calling themselves a 'land girl'. Come on, spill the beans. You're alien, ain't you?" He looked at her face sideways, as though he was afraid she might put a spell on him.

Aquella shook her head fiercely. Her black hair swung round, strands of it flicking the stranger's face. Her eyes blazed.

Billy whipped out his notebook. He'd caught up with one, he was sure of that. He'd only been in Scotland two days and here he was face to face with an alien. Fame and fortune would soon be his. "So tell me, fish girl, where was you born?"

"Here," Aquella said, taking a small step backwards.

"What? On the beach?" He clicked his pen then sniffed, as though smelling her. "Or in the sea? You was, wasn't ya? Fish girl! Ha!" Billy fumbled in his pocket, whipped out his camera and pointed it at Aquella.

Then he shuddered. Through the camera lens he saw how clear her sea-green eyes shone, how small and animal-like her nose was, how not-quite-human her face seemed.

Aquella glared at the camera and bared her teeth. Spying the sharp flash of her teeth Billy Mole gulped. With trembling hands he clicked the switch.

"Right, that's that," he said, though some of his swaggering confidence had gone, "yeah, right then. So that'll be splashed all over London." He glanced at her and took a step back. "You should be happy. You're gonna be famous!" He grinned.

Aquella scowled at him, which quickly wiped the grin from Billy Mole's face. "R-right then... um..." He levelled the camera at the ground. With a snap he took a photo of her feet. "Them's gonna be all over London an all. So – um – fish girl..."

But words had suddenly failed Billy Mole.

Aquella's bright green eyes pierced into his own. She felt a surge of anger shoot through her. Lorelie had said the land wasn't safe. Why wasn't it safe? Because people like this boy had come snooping around. She wanted to turn and flee, but knew she couldn't outrun him.

With shaking fingers Billy Mole opened his notebook, pulled the plastic top off his biro pen, cleared his throat, then said, "So, um... anyway. On with the interview. You ready?"

Aquella continued to glare at him. She took a step back, and another.

"So, right then, tell the world what's it like being a fish."

Suddenly Aquella heard a high-pitched whirring noise zip through the air above her; the kind you hear when a fisherman casts his line. Aquella looked up.

"What the heck's that?" she heard the teenager cry out.

The whirr turned to a hiss. He yelled out. He fell to the ground.

Aquella gasped and stumbled back. The scary teenager was lying in front of her, face down in the sand, wriggling from side to side and yelling, with what looked like a fishing line wrapped around his ankles.

Quick. Behind the gorse bush. Hurry.

Aquella glanced up at the large gorse bush that grew by the beach path. Astounded, she saw the yellow bush shake. With pounding heart and aching legs she fled to the shaking bush. As soon as she was there she dived into the gap Fin had made.

I can't – believe – you actually did – that. Even in selkie-speech she sounded exhausted.

Lucky for you Dad's teaching me how to cast a fishing line. Fin grinned and with a sharp stone cut the line. *Shame is, I've lost Dad's best weight.* Fin picked up the rod.

The haar was so thick now that the teenager tangled in the line was swallowed up in a white cloud. *Do you think he was looking for the kist in the cave?*

No, he's on the hunt for aliens. He wants to write a story, or something like that. He took my photo!

Come on – before he untangles himself. Let's get home.

As they ran Aquella, between pants and gasps, told Magnus Fin how the teenager had jeered and called her fish girl. Fin's face clouded with worry. "He's some kind of a spy," Aquella went on. "He might be the pa-pizza man Tarkin was talking about!"

They had reached the garden when Aquella pulled Fin towards her. "Hey, Fin, that scary teenager made me forget; Lorelie came to see me!"

"Who's Lorelie?"

"She was my good friend when I lived under the sea. She taught me many things. She told me how troubled Neptune is, how strange it is under the water. They're really worried."

Fin twisted his moon-stone around his neck. "Did *he* see her? The stranger on the beach – did he see Lorelie?"

Aquella shrugged. "I don't know. But listen to me, Fin. Lorelie and I were held prisoner together in the false king's palace. We were the monster's favourite singers. For hours and hours we had to sing – ridiculous songs about how he would be king of the land. During those long hours we saw many things. Aquella switched to selkie-speech. *We saw how the great white shark, the monster's bodyguard, kept a set of keys and never let them out of his sight. Perhaps the key to the Seudan was among them; he boasted that it was. Perhaps it's in the palace by his body.*

The great white shark? Fin lingered at the front door. He remembered the awful shark and how, as soon as its master was blinded and writhing in agony, it had made a desperate dive to try and claim stolen treasure for itself. Magnus Fin remembered seeing the shark being crushed in the great banqueting hall.

So that's where the key was: rusting away beside the rotten carcass of the great white shark amongst the ruins of the monster's palace, deep at the bottom of the sea.

She also said she had good news. Aquella pushed open the cottage door, and shrugged. *But I don't know what it is.*

Chapter 19

Back in the Rugged Coast, Billy made a few notes:

Fish girl woddels and was born on beech. Spoke to the sea. Magic powers - out of the air she lassooed me. Billy Mole is close to uncovering the biggest secret ever - alien fish folk are alive and capabel of gr8 evil, hurting innosent folk like me. Mrs Anderson is weird too. And there's weird stuff on the beach. They're all weird.

Billy was propped up on his bed with his sore ankle resting on a pillow. He had a bruise on his elbow, a bruise on his knee and a bruise on his hip. He chewed the end of his pen then made a start on his article.

In the far north are aliens discovered by journalist Billy Mole. They go about in disgise as humans, but I wasn't fooled. They got funny webbed feet and glinty evil eyes and they can fool you cos they are kinda pretty. But they r a danger 2 humans. They tried 2 get me drowned and bound me with a fishing line. They no there secret is out - exposed by Billy Mole. And Billy Mole says get back 2 the sea where they came from in the first place and quit pretending that they're "land people".

Billy Mole sat back, pleased with himself. What a great story. The spell checker would sort out any mistakes. Billy read it over a few times then frowned. The big man would want a bit more than this. Apart from a few words from the fish girl Billy didn't exactly have the exclusive interview yet. He stretched down to rub his sore ankle and his knee and his hip and his elbow. If he was honest he didn't really want to come face to face with the fish girl again. How she had managed to trap him like that he didn't know. She probably had alien powers!

But Magnus Fin – now that's who he wanted to interview. He wanted a photo of the famous eyes. They'd look good in the magazine. And it would be handy to see the parents. Likely they'd be weird too.

Billy looked at his watch. It was six o'clock. He peered out of the window. It wasn't raining. He would saunter down to the house Mrs Anderson had pointed out. With a bit of luck and a bit of cunning, he'd scoop that exclusive interview, add it to his story, email it down to the big man then hop on the next train south.

Billy paced up and down the bedroom, trying to cook up a cunning story for the aliens down by the sea. When an idea finally came to him he tried it out on the mirror. "Good evening," he said in his poshest voice, "you are so not going to believe this but, yes, your address was picked in a prize draw. You and your family are the winners of an all-expenses-paid holiday in sunny Spain. Congratulations! I simply need a few details..."

Billy grinned at the mirror. He turned up his collar, squared his shoulders and narrowed his eyes. Then he rubbed his thumb against his fingers. "The big time's coming, Billy boy," he crooned, strutting out of the room and through the small house. Then Billy Mole was off, scurrying through the village and down to the sea, his cunning story perfecting itself in his mind.

Barbara's face lit up. She flung her hands to her cheeks. "Really? Oh, I don't believe it! A holiday? Oh, how fantastic. How wonderful!"

Billy Mole smiled his sickliest smile. His cunning plan was working a treat. This woman, though, looked perfectly normal – pretty even. Not like a fish at all. Billy glanced over her shoulder. Not seeing anyone around, he carried on with his prepared speech.

"And so, if I could just step inside for a moment or two and take some details, then that dream holiday is yours."

Aquella was out at her band practice. Magnus Fin was upstairs in his room, looking through his treasures. When he heard the voice downstairs he froze. Quickly he got down on his hands and knees and pressed his ear to the floor, the jagged carpet grazing his cheek. "Magnus Fin," he heard, "your son – I'll need a few words with him. You are going to love sunny Spain. So, where is he – your son?"

Fin couldn't believe it. What a cheek! How dare the snooping teenager come to his house? Tarkin had been right about paparazzi. Magnus Fin had to get away. He couldn't risk being caught, for the sake of all the selkies. They'd be captured – put on display – a laughing stock! And to Fin's disbelief his mum seemed to be falling right into the trap.

The mumbling voice went on, "And of course you'll get spending money, yeah, shed loads of it."

"Oh! My husband will be so delighted. He's up helping with the lambs at the moment. He works so hard, but as soon as he gets in I'll tell him. I can't wait. Who would ever guess we would win something? We, of all people. Oh dear, I feel like crying!"

"Yeah, anyway, back to Magnus Fin. Could you go and get him? Bet he's never been abroad before."

"Oh, you're right there, poor laddie. He's hardly been anywhere. No, it hasn't been easy for him. Just wait and I'll call him. Oh goodness, he'll be thrilled."

From upstairs Magnus Fin heard his mother's footsteps patter across the living-room floor and hurry down the hallway. He heard her shout up the stairs, "Magnus! Come on down. Oh son, quick, you are not going to believe this!"

He shot a glance at his bedroom window. Without a sound he got to his feet and tiptoed over to it. Willing the window not to squeak he pushed it open. A rush of cool air hit him. He gulped. He had never tried jumping from his window before. It was high up. He clambered onto the stool beside the window.

"Magnus? Come on down."

The hum of the sea reached Magnus Fin's ears. He grabbed the side of the window and stepped onto the windowsill. He'd have to act fast. His stomach churned.

"Are you there, son?"

Fin's mind raced. He would have to jump, then run to the sea, then warn the selkies. They were being hounded, they really were, and they had to be careful. They would have to flee to Sule Skerrie. They couldn't come ashore any more and leave their seal skins lying about. They'd be in the newspapers, then bus loads of tourists would come hoping to catch a glimpse of them. The magic would be ruined.

Trembling and stooping, Fin manoeuvred himself onto the outside ledge. Once he was out there he stood tall and looked down. He felt sick. Better not look down. He inched along the ledge. He heard his mother coming up the stairs. There was nothing else for it. He had to jump. If he bent his knees and rolled the instant he hit the ground he'd be OK. He hoped so.

The bedroom door swung open. His mother was in his room. "Magnus?"

Sweat ran into his eyes. His pressed the palms of his hands back against the window pane. The glass felt cold and damp. His heart thumped.

"Magnus Fin? Are you in here?"

He jumped. He felt a rush of air past his ears. He felt the whack as his moon-stone hit under his chin. He landed on the grass with a thud, instantly letting his knees collapse. He curled into a ball and rolled over. For a second he lay on the ground, stunned with the shock to his body.

In the house he heard a chair being scraped over the floor, then someone thumping on the living-room window.

"Oi!"

Fin staggered to his feet and ran.

A moment later Barbara appeared back in the living room, shrugging and shaking her head. "He's not there. Perhaps this is his basketball night. I can't remember. I'm so sorry. You've set my mind in a whirl with this holiday news. I still can't believe it!"

Billy Mole tried not to look in a desperate hurry. He side-stepped to the door. "No probs, I'll come back when your husband's home. I'll need his signature. Thanks anyway. See you later. Bye."

Barbara was still shaking her head when Billy Mole hurried out of the house, ran down the garden and raced off along the beach path.

Magnus Fin had never run so fast. He crashed over bracken and sped along the beach path. Thorns caught at his jeans. Sticky willies clung to him. A pheasant squawked and flew up in his face. Fin glanced back over his shoulder. Was the stranger following him? He couldn't see him, but could hear the distant cries of, "Oi! Fish boy!"

Panting hard Magnus Fin reached the skerries and leapt from rock to rock. He heard footsteps snap behind him. "Oi, you! Come 'ere!" Fin saw a white flash of light. Then another. The stranger was taking photographs.

Fin ran on, making for the cave. He kicked off his shoes as he ran. Thoughts clawed at his brain. What if this stranger told their story? What if television cameras came up here? Then what? Would the selkies be sold off? Or gaped at in a zoo? Fin had to warn them. The stranger may have caught Aquella, but he wasn't going to catch Magnus Fin.

By this time he was nearly at the cave. He knew what he needed to do when he got there, and he grasped his moon-stone for the courage to do it.

Magnus Fin disappeared into the darkness of the cave. Quickly he checked on the box, hidden under a tangle of dried seaweed. It was still there, safe from prying eyes. Then he tugged his red hoodie over his head, pulled off his jeans and scaled the rock, his strong webbed feet finding footholds. In moments he was at the top and felt on the ledge for his seal skin. His hand fell upon the warm fur. This soft fur felt like a part of him. It was – it was his seal skin. The bat that had been using it as a bed flew off. Fin shook out his seal skin, shimmied down to the sandy floor then gazed at the black pelt.

Outside he could hear the stranger stumbling over the rocks. "Do it, Fin," he coaxed himself. "Step into in and let the change happen. There's no time to lose. Quick!" And he did.

"Just you wait, fish boy. I'm going to get your weird story. What a scoop! I didn't come a thousand miles for nothing you know!"

Magnus Fin hauled himself over the smooth pebbles. They shifted and crunched down under his strong seal body. With his front flippers he pushed himself forward. He was almost at the shore. Fin turned his seal face to see the stranger stumble on the beach. He could see him properly now. He only looked about sixteen and, Fin was sure by the way the boy staggered over the stones, he had never been on a beach before.

With one almighty push Magnus Fin slipped into the North Sea, flipped back his tail fins and swam away. While back on the beach, at the mouth of the cave, Billy

Mole shouted into the gaping darkness, "Hey, fish boy! I know you're in there! Come on out and talk to me. The secret's out."

Of course, Magnus Fin wasn't in there, but on the sandy floor of the cave his clothes were.

"You can't fool me." Billy Mole took a hesitant step into the cave. "It's only an interview I'm after. Like, what's the fuss? Don't you get it? You're gonna be a celebrity!" He took another step. It smelt damp. He didn't like it. He forced himself to take one more step, stood on a shell, smashed it and at the same time a bat swooped down and brushed his face. Billy screamed and staggered back. "Hey, no tricks, fish boy." Billy was back at the mouth of the cave. "I'll wait here." Billy sat on a stone and waited. He amused himself by placing an empty can on a rock and trying to hit it. Still Magnus Fin didn't appear.

Only after Billy Mole grew bored with hitting the can and sitting on the stone did he force himself to take another look inside the cave. That's when he found the red hoodie and the jeans. The boy he'd been chasing had been wearing a red hoodie and jeans. Billy kicked the wall of the cave. He peered out to sea and finally had to admit to himself that Magnus Fin had given him the slip.

"So, fish boy went for a swim, did he?" Billy scratched his head and shuddered at the thought of ice-cold water. There was no way Billy Mole was going to dive into that shark-infested ocean and get mauled to death. "I'll wait right here," he yelled to the sea ahead of him. "Cos Billy Mole's gonna get you, fish boy! One way or the other, Billy Mole's gonna get your secret! Then Billy Mole here's gonna tell the world!"

Chapter 20

It took Magnus Fin a while to feel comfortable. He had only worn his seal skin once before – when he went all the way to Sule Skerrie with medicine for Miranda last autumn. It hadn't been easy to take the seal skin off afterwards. He thought he'd never find his way back to being a boy. Because of that he'd been scared to put his seal skin on again, and for months it lay gathering dust in the cave.

Fin swam on into the deep water. Miranda was right; the sea felt lost. At times deep currents dragged him then pushed him on. Even the fish that glided by seemed confused. Magnus Fin turned and twisted. He flipped a somersault, trying to shake off the gloomy mood of the sea. A salmon darted past. In a flash Fin bared his sharp teeth, flicked his powerful tail fins and was after it.

The salmon was fast, but Magnus Fin was faster. He closed his jaws over the fish, snapped down and crunched into the bones. He chewed and swallowed, tossing away the bony skeleton. Magnus Fin felt the salty goodness of the meat flood his body. He was animal – alert, strong and brave.

Fin rose to the surface and lifted his black shiny head from the water. He focused on the distant shore where, sitting on a rock, flinging stones, was the scary teenager.

Except he didn't look so scary any more. In fact, now that Magnus Fin was a seal, the teenager didn't look scary at all. Fin heard him yell, "Come on out and talk to me, fish boy! I'm waiting."

Fin lowered his head, turned and plunged down through the water. *Wait as long as you like,* thought Fin, twisting in and out between thick arms of seaweed, *fish boy isn't there!*

The sight of sea anemones, luminescent jellyfish with tentacles as long as spaghetti, side-scuttling crabs and shoals of needle-like fish mesmerised Magnus Fin. He could gaze at them for ever, and for a while he did, until he remembered why he had risked wearing his seal skin. The selkie secret! Suddenly he was filled with a sense of urgency. He had to protect it! He had to warn his selkie family not to come to the beach. The paparazzi were after them!

He circled slowly, trying to sense the whereabouts of the selkies. He lifted his nose up then down, right then left. The small band of selkies, led by his grandmother Miranda, lived in this very bay in the far north of Scotland. This had been their home for generations, but perhaps not for much longer if the teenager got his way. The sea boomed. Huge kelp fronds swayed beneath him. They tickled his belly as he nosed forwards, exploring the world with his whiskers. Below him, a blue lobster scuttled under a rock. Magnus Fin dipped downwards, swishing his tail fins back and forth. The deep ocean was a hazy blur of dark shapes and shadows. He swam on until he thought he could hear a creature singing. Fin followed the muffled sound. As he glided onwards the sound grew louder. His selkie family were close, for only a selkie could sing like that.

Deeper he swam, through dark kelp forests and over sprawling mossy boulders, until he came to a cavern pitted with barnacles. The song was loud and clear now. If this scary teenager succeeded in telling the world the secret of the selkies then there would be no more songs like this. Weighed down by an awful sadness Fin flicked his hind fins from side to side, splaying his flippers to slow down.

As he reached the inner chamber of the cavern Fin paused. At the same moment the singing came to an end and everything was silent, even the booming of the distant waves against the rocks grew quiet. Then splashing yelps and claps erupted. Quickly now Fin swam on, pushing his nose through a swirling curtain of seaweed. He blinked. His whiskers brushed up against decorations of shells and sea grass. In front of him a party of seals tumbled and twisted. The seals, Fin realised, were dancing! He had swum right into a selkie party!

Believing in the power of song, the selkies danced and sang to help every occasion. This was to help the sea, to help Neptune restore his wisdom, and to bring back joy. Miranda told Fin all this as she swam up to him, nuzzling him in welcome. *Ceud mile fàilte, Magnus Fin. You followed our songs? Oh Fin, sometimes all we can do is sing. Look how it brightens us.*

Caught up in the festivities, Fin, for a moment, forgot the teenager. Soon more and more seals swam over to greet him. They were always happy to see Magnus Fin, this brave child of both worlds. Fin recognised Shuna and Ondine. Behind them, strong and handsome, came his Uncle Coll. And then others who nodded in greeting, nuzzled him gently and spoke their names: *Erla, Ruiraigh, Catriona, Sylva.* The names swam in his mind as the selkies tumbled and twisted around him.

Come and meet my sweetheart, said Ronan, nudging him over to a cove draped with clam shells. Fin tumbled with Ronan and they splashed flippers together. *Isn't she beautiful?*

Lorelie, Ronan's sweetheart, lay on a mossy stone. She lifted her head, and seeing Magnus Fin lifted a flipper and waved. She was black, fat and glossy, with shining brown eyes. *Fàilte, Magnus Fin,* she said, floating up from the stone to greet him. At that moment another selkie began to sing while others twisted and tumbled in the water. Lorelie danced with Ronan, and Miranda swam over to dance with her grandson. Even the seaweed fronds, swaying back and forth, seemed to dance.

It would have been the easiest thing in the world to twist and tumble in the cool water and forget. Forget that the great ruler of the seas had forgotten how to rule. Forget that King Neptune needed to have his treasures of wisdom returned to him. Forget that on the shore a snooping journalist wanted to tell the world about the alien fish folk. But Magnus Fin couldn't forget. He didn't know how to break the news. Around him the dancing went on.

I tried to find you, said Ronan, swimming close to him. *I thought I'd find you treasure hunting on the beach.* Ronan swayed as he spoke. *I took my seal coat off and waited for you on the beach. But you weren't there. Then a human came with a big stick, and I had to flee. But I was there for ages. I came close to the house.*

Worry flashed in Fin's eyes. *You shouldn't do that,* he said. *You must be careful.*

Lorelie swam up to Ronan and nuzzled him as the party whirled around them. Magnus Fin watched as Ronan and Lorelie danced together. He wished he could join in with the mood of the party, but he couldn't. Worse than that, he was going to break it up.

Miranda noticed his awkwardness. Fin saw a dark shadow of worry flit across her face. *Did you hide the treasure?* she asked, swimming close to him.

Yes, it's in the cave. But look, Miranda, there's something else...

Miranda flashed a look at his flippers. *Your hands? They are fine, I trust? Did you wrap the kist in kelp as I asked you?*

Magnus Fin nodded. *I did.* He twisted in the water. All around him seal bodies swayed and turned. The cave flashed into Fin's mind, and with it the image of the boy with the black jacket. It wasn't only the kist Fin had to guard, it was the selkie secret. He had to warn them! He concentrated hard to push his thoughts out loudly to everyone at the same time.

Listen everyone, please, I have come to warn you of danger. Now every seal turned to face him. The singing died away. Fin went on, his mighty seal heart pounding in his chest. *Some land people have suspicions. Some land people seem to guess that Aquella and I are, well, fish folk. Aliens, that's what they're saying. And they have cameras, and they want to tell the selkie story, and hunt you down. Miranda has asked me to guard your secret. It's my secret too.*

127

It's my dad's secret. It's Aquella's secret. But I have come to ask you to be careful. Don't come ashore. Don't leave your seal skins lying around.

But what about the solstice celebrations? Lorelie asked. *We've always had our party on the beach. And it's going to be extra special this year. Ronan and I are getting married!*

Wow, that's amazing news. It might blow over by then, Fin replied. *This boy that seems to be after us – he won't stay for ever.* Magnus Fin hoped not, though in reality he had no idea what the boy would do.

By now every seal had gathered close, their large kind eyes staring at Magnus Fin. Fin gazed at them and swallowed hard. He couldn't let harm come to them. *I will try and convince him not to tell our secret. Believe me, I will try.*

Magnus Fin speaks wisely, Miranda said. *And so, we will go away for a while.* She turned to face her grandson. *We do not want to draw attention to you and Aquella. We want to help you. We will go to Sule Skerrie. There we will be safe from prying eyes.* Fin felt a great welling up of sadness. Sule Skerrie was a long and lonely way away, under the Arctic rim.

Miranda sensed his concern. *We will leave but we will return. When it is safe again, for you – and for us – then we will return. And I will listen for your call. If you need me, I will come.*

Then Miranda swam close to Magnus Fin, nuzzling her head gently against his. *Soon the great lantern in the sky shines bright. It will help you work your sea magic. These are difficult times and there is so much to do. The crab told me you must go to the sunken ship near the kelp forest, where you will find help. Find the key, Fin. Then, when I give you a sign, return the treasure to Neptune. Then, and only then, order will be restored.*

Fin shuddered at the thought of the quest that lay ahead. At least now he knew where to start.

Miranda looked at him, her beautiful white head soft with concern. *You can do it,* she whispered. Then she turned from him and gathered up her people. Fin could only watch as she nuzzled every other seal and guided them out of the cavern. Fin heard her words float faintly towards him – *Tioraidh an-dràsta, Magnus Fin* – farewell.

Chapter 21

Feeling like the loneliest seal in the world, Magnus Fin hauled himself up the stony beach, and on his belly slid over pebbles, sand and seaweed towards the cave. Miranda's words echoed in his mind: *Go to the sunken ship.*

As Fin rocked over tangles of seaweed he wondered, with a shudder, who or what he might find in the sunken ship. Earlier he had longed to explore there. Now he wasn't so sure. He felt so tired. He splayed his strong flippers on to the springy seaweed and dragged himself forward. It was still light. Fin felt the early evening sun warm his back. It was pleasant being a seal. He was in no rush to drag himself into the cave, take off his seal skin and change back into his human form. He lay near the entrance to the cave for a moment, lowering his sleek black head onto a tangle of pungent seaweed. The moon-stone, which even as a seal he wore on a leather lace around his neck, nestled in amongst the red and green tangles. He breathed in the strong smell, feeling his whole body relax. All he wanted to do was sleep.

As sluggish waves lapped at his back and a few crows cawed on the hillside Magnus Fin slept. He had forgotten how what feels like hours spent in the selkie world can be just a few minutes on land. So he didn't hear the boy in the black jacket enter the cave. He didn't hear him hiss into the darkness, "Think you're gonna give Billy Mole the slip? Think again, fish boy." He didn't hear Billy Mole stumble in the darkness of the cave and trip up. He didn't hear him scramble to his feet, muttering, "What's this then? Interesting! Very interesting!" He didn't hear Billy Mole hit the interesting thing and rattle it, and shake it, and thump it, and prod and pry. He didn't hear him grab the lid and yank it.

What he did hear was a piercing scream. It cut into his slumber like a knife. Startled, Magnus Fin opened his eyes. He jolted his head up from his seaweed pillow. Was he dreaming? Another scream tore the air. Fin slithered forward. He rocked and bounced towards the cave, then stopped.

The boy came reeling out of the cave, grasping his hand and howling in agony. "Help!" he shrieked. "Somebody help me!"

Magnus Fin knew instantly what had happened. The stranger had tried to open the kist. Fin stared at the howling teenager, who turned and locked eyes with the seal. The seal had one green eye, one brown eye and a moon-stone around his neck. Fin's eyes fell to the boy's hand. It had swollen. It was bleeding.

In a flash Magnus Fin swung round, rocked furiously over the stones and slipped back into the sea. He swam as fast as he could, slicing through the slack water. He remembered the way to the northern kelp forest and in no time was there. Plunging down amongst the dusky brown fronds he tore up fat strands of kelp with his teeth.

With the strands trailing from his mouth he turned towards the coast and sped back through the water. As he broke the surface he heard the whimpers and wails of the teenager who was now crouching on the beach, gripping his swollen hand and rocking back and forth.

Fin hauled up the beach. He felt a pebble land on his back, then another and another. With his good hand the teenager was pelting him. Magnus Fin howled and rocked faster, dragging himself closer and closer to the boy.

Billy Mole stared, horrified, as a black seal approached him. He let the pebble fall. He screamed. He tried to get up but his knees buckled under him.

Pushing down with his flippers Magnus Fin raised his head up and stared at the trembling teenager, who from that moment on was powerless to move. Nor could he peel his eyes away. He could only stare and stare, as a black seal with hypnotic mismatched eyes approached him and, with a flipper which looked uncannily like a hand, wrapped slimy stuff around the teenager's swollen hand.

No scream came from Billy Mole. His jaw fell. His skin paled. His whole body trembled uncontrollably. When the kelp bandage was fastened, the black seal slid quickly away.

When Magnus Fin, five minutes later, wearing his red hoodie and jeans, covered the kist once more with the seaweed disguise, ran out of the cave and scrambled up the hillside, the teenager in the black jacket was still sitting on the beach in shock, staring at his hand.

"Tarkin!"

Tarkin dropped the book he was reading. His whole body tightened. He didn't like his mother's tone of voice, not one bit. He didn't answer.

"I said Tarkin!"

"I'm busy," he mumbled. He jumped off his bed and fumbled for the book. He had to look busy. *Let it not be the necklace – please!*

"I want to talk to you and right now; I don't care if you're busy. Come on through here this instant."

Tarkin couldn't believe it. How come his mother suddenly missed the necklace? He took it days ago. Why now? His mind raced. Maybe it wasn't the necklace she was mad about? Maybe he'd done something else wrong? He racked his brains. What could it be?

"Now!"

She sounded seriously angry. Tarkin stood up and went to his bedroom door. His heart thumped. His mother was never like this. She usually sang pop songs, and called him honey. It scared him. He crept through to the kitchen, quaking, as if he was walking the gangplank like the boy in his book. He took a deep breath, then opened the kitchen door. His mother was standing by the breakfast bar, her hands on her hips and her thick blonde hair spilling from its tartan ribbon. Her face was red. She looked as though she would explode.

"Well?" she said, her whole body shaking.

"Well what?" Tarkin replied in a quiet voice. He looked down at the floor, at the grainy pattern in the wood.

"Don't 'well what' me. You know perfectly well what. Did you or did you not take my pearl necklace?"

Tarkin mumbled, still studying the floor. "Dunno what you're talking about."

Martha sighed loudly then marched over, took his chin in her hand and thrust his face upwards, forcing him to look at her. "I'm talking about my precious necklace. It's gone! I've looked everywhere. Frank sure didn't take it. No one's been in the house. That was my mother's necklace. One of the few things I have that belonged to her. Where is it?" Her voice rose. Her eyes filled with tears. Her grip on Tarkin's chin tightened. "Where is it? Tell me!"

"Ow!" he said, trying to pull away. "You're hurting me. Could be a magpie took it? I dunno."

Martha let him go, pulled back a chair and sank into it. She buried her head in her hands, sighed again then looked up at her son, who was standing in the middle of the floor, rubbing his chin. In a steady voice, as though trying hard to control herself, she said, "No Tarkin. I don't think a magpie took it. I need you to tell me the truth. No frills. No fancy made-up stories. No once-upon-a-time stuff. The truth. That's all I want. The plain truth."

Tarkin looked at her. He twisted his earring. He coughed. He coiled his long hair around his finger. Then he said quietly, "I wanted to give it to my mermaid."

On the tiny island of Sule Skerrie, under the Arctic rim, the selkies gathered. The raw lonely beauty of their ancestral home lay long miles from human habitation, and many grey seals had already come to seek peace on its isolated rocks.

Exhausted, the selkies, after their long swim from the bay, hauled up and found resting places next to these grey seals. They nodded to each other. They gave a honk or a weary howl in greeting. But selkies are not seals – not completely. With their seal coat wrapped about them they look like seals. Wearing their human skin they look like humans. The grey seals grunted then dragged their tired bodies over the rock to make room for the visitors, but they had no tongue for selkie-speech. They closed their eyes and slept.

But for the selkies sleep didn't come so easily. While they lay cold on the rocks of Sule Skerrie, they longed for the bay of their home. They yearned to be close to humans, to join in their games, play on the shore and call to them from quiet caves. They yearned to hear Magnus Fin serenade them with his penny whistle, to see Ragnor walk along the shore, to hear Aquella sing.

This rock in the northern Atlantic was one of the loneliest places on the planet. To the north lay the ice and snow of the Arctic. About them, wind howled. Grey harsh waves broke over the rocks. After their long journey the selkies huddled together, exhausted and confused. It was a cold and lonely place, but it was safe.

Ronan was more dejected than anyone. *But our wedding, the party on the beach... What about that?* He asked Miranda, pressing close to Lorelie to keep her warm.

Miranda had no answer. She lay by his other side, nestling close for warmth. The Arctic gale moaned about the lonely island. Ronan lifted his head and howled into the moaning wind. Waves crashed against the rock and hurled spray high into the air. It was the month of June but cold like mid-winter.

Chapter 22

The moon shone so bright through his window, Magnus Fin couldn't sleep that night. Not a wink. It seemed like hours he lay awake, going over and over in his mind the events of the past few days: the stranger in the black jacket; Tarkin and his imaginary mermaid, but maybe she wasn't imaginary; then of course the thing in the sand that was now in the cave – Neptune's stolen treasure. And what would he find in the sunken ship? Fin felt a thrill at the thought of diving to the sunken ship.

The clock downstairs struck four in the morning. Fin counted the chimes. Every chime urged him to rise. The moon that Miranda had called the great lantern in the sky had reached its fullness. Fin remembered too with a shiver that Neptune, without the Seudan, would not last another moon.

Magnus Fin couldn't lie in bed any longer. He got up and opened his bedroom window, letting in the hum of the sea. The image of the rusty box hidden under the clump of seaweed wouldn't leave him. Neptune needed it back. Maybe the snooping teenager would go back for it? Or maybe he'd report it? There was no telling what the strange boy would do. Fin leant out of the window and breathed in the cold salty air. The sea called him. The great lantern in the sky called him. At four o'clock that morning, finding the key and returning the treasure to Neptune seemed like the most important thing in the world.

Magnus Fin, as a child of both worlds, had choices. He could travel in the water as a seal. He could travel as a boy. He grasped his moon-stone. *Boy*, it seemed to say. Fin looked at his hands. His long fingers would help him find a small key. He looked at his comfortable boat-bed. Who in their right mind would swap a warm bed for the cold sea? Going into the sea at four in the morning was a mad idea. It was crazy. But when you were half-selkie, mad and crazy were sometimes right.

Fin tiptoed to his wardrobe and quietly opened it. In the dark he fumbled for the rubbery feel of his wetsuit. He pulled it out and struggled into it. It felt tight under the arms. Fin tugged at the sleeves. He grinned to himself and looked down at his lanky legs; this was a fine time to learn he had grown!

At that moment he heard a creak on the stair. He froze. Was somebody up? If his mother discovered him she'd never let him go out at this time. Fin held his breath while his door handle turned and slowly the door opened. Aquella stood silhouetted in the moonlight. She wore her baggy white pyjamas and clutched a ragged old teddy.

"Be careful," she whispered. "I know you have to go. I know the selkies need you; you're the only one who can return the treasure. But be careful – please." Aquella took a step forward. "I can't believe you're going back to the ruins of that awful monster's palace. I'd go if I could."

Fin didn't want to return there either, but he did want to help King Neptune. He pulled his trainers out from under his bed and slipped his feet into them, then smiled at his cousin. He wanted her to at least feel he was confident, even if he wasn't. He'd been on missions under the sea before and he'd always come back, hadn't he?

"You not going to wish me luck then?" he whispered, standing up now and rubbing his moon-stone.

Good luck, she said in selkie-speech. *The bones of the great white shark may be near the shattered throne. And amongst the bones you'll find the key. The key is small – hardly the size of your little finger. I'm so proud of you, Magnus Fin, and I'll sing for you. It's all I can do.*

Thanks. With his green eye he winked at her. Then Magnus Fin crept out of his room and down the stairs. Without a sound he opened the front door then slipped out into the darkness.

Aquella meanwhile padded back to her tiny attic room. But she didn't go back to bed. She pulled on her puffy jacket over her pyjamas. She put on warm socks then wellington boots, a hat and wrapped a scarf around her neck. Then she too crept downstairs and slipped out into the night.

In the silvery moonlight Aquella followed the soft imprints of her cousin's steps. Hurrying along the beach path she rounded the coast. Immediately she spotted the dark shape of Magnus Fin silhouetted on the edge of the rocks. She saw him bend his knees and stretch back his arms. She felt her heart flutter. She saw him leap from the rock. Then she heard a splash. He was gone.

For a while Aquella gazed after him. "Neptune guide you and protect you," she murmured into the shadowy darkness. She found herself a soft patch of sand at the edge of the beach and sat down, hugging her knees for warmth. From here, safe from salt water, she could survey the moonlit sea. From the hill behind her the *tu-woo* of a night owl kept her company. Soon the first glimmer of daylight would appear over the eastern horizon. And soon – all being well – Magnus Fin would return, shaking seawater from his hair, grinning, and clutching in his hand the key to Neptune's treasure chest!

As she waited she let her fingers stroke the cool sand. She lifted the sand then let it run out slowly between her fingers. As the sand fell she sang. It was a Gaelic song about a fisherman who was lost at sea. Had anyone heard her sing they'd believe that she knew what that felt like – to be lost at sea.

When her song was done she half opened her eyes and peered over her shoulder towards the cave. There were surely a few bats, perhaps a rat, or even a deer snuggled up next to the rusty old kist that lay in that cave. Little did these creatures know the great power of the treasure they slept next to.

The night was still. Aquella shivered and looked anxiously along the beach path. If the snooping teenager came back she didn't know what she would do. Magnus Fin was not here to spin a fishing line around his ankles. But somehow she didn't think he would come back – not at four o'clock in the morning. Normal folk didn't go to the beach at four o'clock in the morning.

Aquella turned back to face the sea. Through her long black eyelashes she could see the first chink of dawn. She sang again. What else could she do? This was her way of helping Magnus Fin. This was her way of guarding the Seudan. She sang with all her selkie heart, because there were few places under the ocean worse than the false king's ruined palace.

Chapter 23

Magnus Fin, jumping into the dark sea, felt the rush of cool water. He tilted his body forward and groped for the doorway. His hand closed over the familiar curved shape of the shell handle. He pulled. The emerald-green light flashed from the crack in the rock door. The rock door opened wider, water gushed with the force of it, then he was through – into the magical world of the selkies.

Magnus Fin twisted round to gaze at the swaying world he had entered. Bars of light, streaming down from the moonlight above, bent in the water. Glancing up, silver patterns shimmered and shifted on the surface. Beneath him long swathes of seaweed, like weary dancers, drifted from side to side. Magnus Fin stretched out his arms and swam. A shoal of curious fish glided towards him then darted off in all directions.

Fin blinked, letting a thin beam of light seep from his eyes; his underwater vision shone like torchlight through the darkness. Balls of red seaweed rolled over the plankton beneath him. He dived, picked up a seaweed ball, threw it and watched its slow-motion curve.

Fin felt the familiar surge of sea-excitement. Even if the sea was suffering, there was still much to wonder at. But he shook himself. If he was going to find the sunken ship he couldn't spend ages hurling balls of seaweed.

So he swam on to where the underwater world turned dark green. Slimy seaweed brushed his face and feet. Magnus Fin shuddered, grasped his moon-stone, and paddled off fast.

The sunken ship, he remembered, lay on the ocean floor not far from the northern kelp forest. Only hours earlier, Fin, as a seal, had made the speedy journey there. A thrill of anticipation shot through him. There was nothing Magnus Fin liked better than a sunken ship to explore. He pushed his arms forwards and with fast, wide strokes made good headway.

The wetsuit kept him warm, even if it was a bit small. Fin swam past floating shoals of fish that appeared to be asleep. There were some queer looking creatures in the sea. Fin couldn't help but stare. One odd fish, resembling a toothless old woman with a gaping mouth and sunken cheeks, floated in the water, its bulging eyes shifting from side to side. Underwater vision lent everything a fuzzy haze. Shapes, large and small, appeared out of the dim water then mysteriously disappeared. Sea creatures emerged from rocky crevices, vanished between fronds, or burrowed into the sand.

On and on he swam, his arms slicing through the water, his feet kicking back at a great rate. A prowling greyish bulk appeared from the dim watery world. It roamed the sea ahead before vanishing into the distance, leaving Fin haunted by the unpleasant thought of great white sharks. He grabbed hold of his moon-stone and felt courage pour into him. Trying not to think about starving great whites Magnus Fin ventured on.

But venturing on wasn't so easy. Strong currents dragged him back then pushed him forward. Under him Fin saw piles of smashed shells and carcasses of shattered lobsters. In the unblinking round eyes of passing fish Magnus Fin saw startled fear. The sea was living in confusion. Fin swam faster, thrusting back his webbed feet with urgent kicks. Below him the ocean floor fell downwards like a gaping canyon. Into this he dived, to where the sea lived in perpetual night.

Shining his eye-lights full strength Magnus Fin followed the route Miranda had taken him. Yellow sea grasses, as though knowing his quest, shivered and waved as he passed. Through it all the muffled drone of the sea moaned and boomed. Fin swam over the ribbed sandy plains where lobster creels sat, fastened to long swaying ropes; where spars of rusting iron lay, encrusted with barnacles; where red sea anemones stretched up their thousand spiky fingers and dead men's fingers pointed the way.

Magnus Fin pushed on against the dragging weight of the sluggish sea. His arms were aching, his legs felt like lead. But he was close to the sunken ship, he was sure of it. Forward, his marine instinct guided him. With a sense of foreboding he ventured on into the eerie depths.

Suddenly from out of the watery dimness a massive shape loomed towards him. Fin was ready to turn and swim away when it fractured into a million tiny fish. These fish parted, like silver curtains opening, revealing a slumped and shadowy bulk.

His heart thudded against his ribs. Could this be the sunken ship?

Slowly now he swam towards it. As he drew nearer, crabs scuttled sideways and fish darted into the murk. With slow wide strokes Magnus Fin glided above the dark shape and looked down. It was a ship, he was sure about that – or had been, once upon a time. A water snake uncoiled from round a rusting iron pole and slunk off. Where the snake had been a flag uncurled. Fin's eyes lit on the ragged flag of the skull and crossbones. His pulse raced. He'd come to a sunken pirate ship! He didn't know whether to be terrified or delighted. What, he wondered, treading water and glancing nervously from side to side, was he supposed to do now?

He studied the rotting hull below him. He gaped at the barnacle-encrusted iron bars, the split planks and rotting masts. He could hardly believe it; he was hovering above a pirate ship that must have lain in this watery cemetery for two or three hundred years.

The wreck was half hidden by barnacles, slimy moss and seaweed. Fin grasped a long tuber. Using the stalk as a rope he lowered himself, hand under hand, downwards. Excitement made his fingers tremble. The broken ship was so embedded in sand it didn't move like everything else in the sea. It had made its last voyage a long time ago. What, Fin wondered, had happened to the pirates? The ones who were on board when this very ship went down. Fin let go of his tuber and swam cautiously around the eerie wreck, sweeping his eye-lights over the abandoned vessel.

Stretching out his hand Fin touched the ragged flag, still tied to the broken end of a rusty pole. It felt slimy. He winced. The sunken ship creaked. In such eerie gloom anyone would think (Magnus Fin tried not to think) that such a place would be haunted.

Sea ghosts! the nightmarish thought wormed into his brain. *Sea ghosts!* it screeched. Fin kicked his foot against a spar of wood, causing the wreck to creak mournfully once more. Fin's heart raced. He didn't believe in ghosts, at least not the scary kind. Tarkin did, but Tarkin believed in everything. The thought wouldn't go away. It grew bigger. Forget hungry great white sharks with supersonic electro receptors! Now he was haunted by pirate sea ghosts!

Fin blinked quickly to stop the light streaming from his eyes. If there were pirate sea ghosts slumbering in this ship he didn't want to disturb them. But wasn't he supposed to find help here? Plunged into murky darkness Fin couldn't see the pirate ship now. Only the white from the skull and crossbones glinted. He reached out his hands and groped what felt like the rigging. At the same time something nuzzled him on the back of his neck.

If it was possible to scream at the bottom of the sea, he would have screamed then. It would have been a scream to waken dead sailors. But it wasn't possible to scream, so he didn't. He swung round instead, ready to punch and kick.

Magnus Fin thrashed his arms through the water. He kicked out. Something had touched him. Was it a shark? The touch had been eerily cold, more of an impression than a real touch. Fin's heart batted wildly. Could it be... a sea ghost? He tried to swim away, but his arms felt weak. He didn't know where to go. His stomach churned. The horrible thought clawed at him. Had a sea ghost, in this sunken ship, touched him on the neck? He wriggled backwards. In the murky water all he could see was a dark shadow. And this mysterious shadow was moving towards him.

Nightmare – never ends. You come to torture me? Again?

Fin's hand hit out, but nothing was there. Nothing he could touch. The shadow swirled in the water. It made his skin bristle with fear. The water trembled. Dry jabbing thoughts knocked on his skull.

Nightmare. Endless – nightmare – on and on and so I can never forget. Nev-er!

The anguished voice bore into him. Fin spun round in the water but nothing was there. Fin felt his blood run cold.

The eternal suffering. Release me!

Fin panicked. Selkies would never speak like that. What was it?

The ghost voice went on. *Bad. All bad and to never forget it. Never. Nightmare without end. So many smashed crabs, slaughtered shrimps, tortured fish, imprisoned selkies... And what did we do? We laughed. Laughed and laughed. Now what? You come – come to laugh? At this agony? Death doesn't want me. Though I yearn for it.*

Magnus Fin's eyes, used to the murky dark now, detected a faint shape moving in the water. The agonised words were surely coming from this shadow, which rose up from the bowels of the sunken ship like a snake to the charmer's flute. Gaping at the ghostly slinking shadow Fin pushed frantically back, but found himself wedged against a spar of the ship. Dumbfounded he stared as the shape slunk up and up, displaying its enormous height. Fin swallowed hard. He'd read enough books about the sea to recognise that this shadow snaking through the water was none other than a monstrous conger eel.

Or – his stomach churned, his heart missed a beat – the ghost of a conger eel.

Fin knew eels well. He'd spent ages reading about them – these snake-like monsters that can grow to three metres. Pictures of strong jaws and sharp teeth flashed through his mind. Congers will eat anything, his book said – especially at night! Fin grasped his moon-stone and realised with relief that this conger eel had no teeth to eat with, no powerful jaw. This was a ghost!

Spurred on by a sense of urgency Magnus Fin forced himself to speak to the ghost: *Miranda, my grandmother, said you would help me. I am looking for the key to the Seudan.*

The conger eel seemed to vanish then. The water ruffled. The sunken ship creaked. Then the long shape took form again, the way a shadow grows when the sun comes out.

Me? Help? I kill. I destroy. I lie. I cheat. Now I suffer the endless night. I don't help.

Treading water and breathing deeply Fin tried to find the eyes of the conger. But there were no eyes, only a writhing shadow. Maybe Miranda had got it wrong? Maybe she too, like Neptune, was confused? Or was there some other creature in this sunken ship that might help him? Frantically Fin scanned his torch-lights across the wreck. But nothing stirred – only the monstrous shadow of this tortured creature. Miranda must have meant him.

I am asking for your help, Fin said. *And there is no time to waste.*

Time? I am condemned to eternity with no sleep. Only memories. Smashed skulls, blood and empty laughter. Over and over. Blood and bones and agony.

146

In a flash it became clear to Magnus Fin. He marvelled at Miranda's cleverness. Not for nothing was his grandmother queen of the selkies.

So, Fin said, *you are familiar with the palace of the false king?*

At the name of the false king the shape shuddered then vanished. It emerged moments later behind Magnus Fin. Fin twisted round, sensing the cold presence at his back. He kicked his heels and lurched away from it. Frantically Fin grasped the mast and clung to the slimy flag. The eel uttered pained, strange noises. Fin knew his instinct was right. This massive creature had probably been one of the false king's cruel henchmen. Feeling a surge of courage Magnus Fin took command.

This could be your chance for freedom.

Freedom? the tortured shadow cried. *Freedom is for the good. Freedom doesn't come to the murderers – only nightmare with no end.*

But if you help me it might. Show me the way to the ruins of the false king's palace. Guide me to the ruins of the throne room. Help me find the key, then King Neptune might show pity, he might release you.

The massive shadow of the eel slithered downwards. It slunk in and out between spars of broken ship. It wound its shadowy shape around the barnacle-crusted wheel. It slithered under a chair that was still, miraculously, intact. It undulated along the peeling lettering on the boat's hull. *Beelzebub,* it said.

Seeing the ship's name Fin recoiled. Wasn't it enough that he'd come to a pirate ship? To be in a ship that had the name of the devil only made things worse. The ghostly eel hovered above the slumped statue

147

of a mermaid that lay face down in the sand. She'd once been, Fin guessed, the ship's figurehead. Now her arm was broken, her long golden hair was green. The ghostly eel slid down to lie motionless beside this broken mascot. Was the conger, Fin wondered, asking her advice?

Please help, Magnus Fin wished, *please!*

Then the dry words came, groaning from the broken hull. *I'll help. She says I should help. But I warn you: you might get more than you bargained for.* The shadowy form then rose quickly from the sunken ship and glided snake-like through the murky water.

Magnus Fin kicked back his heels, and followed it.

Chapter 24

Soon the gloom of the sunken ship was far behind. Magnus Fin cut through the ocean, following in the wake of the conger eel. It sucked him along. It darkened the ocean. Even with his torch-lights on full strength, Fin could see little more of his guide than an eerie slinking shadow.

Judging by the route, this ghost, Fin guessed, knew a short cut to the monster's palace. It took sudden quick turns and led Fin down twisting rocky corridors and through caves where salty stalactites hung like daggers. Sometimes the shadowy form took shape. Sometimes it vanished. Kicking back water, Fin followed. Aghast, he watched the ghost swim right through the pointed stalactites. Magnus Fin, flesh, blood and fully alive, needed to duck and dive to avoid them.

Plunging on, Fin's thoughts sped back to that crumbling awful palace at the bottom of the sea. Again he saw blood spurting from the monster's eye, he heard the terrible shriek of the dying creature, he saw again the ridiculous necklace of tin cans and junk that the creature wore, calling it jewellery – when all the time the greatest of all jewels lay under lock and key in that secret stolen kist.

Engrossed in his memories Magnus Fin didn't notice the water had grown murky. He didn't notice the gloom and floating debris above and around him. He bumped his head up against a fallen pillar.

Here, grunted the ghostly eel.

Ouch! cried Magnus Fin.

He shook himself from his memories, and rubbed his head. He hadn't expected to arrive so quickly. He grasped his moon-stone to still his thumping heart, and looked ahead. Even with the courage of his stone he wanted to turn and flee. Through the murky water he could see the ruins of the monster's palace. Marble columns lay slumped on their side, covered in barnacles and moss. Remnants of rubbish, of which the monster was so fond, still floated around. Though much had been cleaned by Neptune's many sea-storms, some remained: a few cans, plastic bottles, crisp packets, rubber gloves, ropes. Fin tightened his grip on the moon-stone. A ghostly silence hung about the ruins and a prickle of fear slithered down his spine.

Ugly. Messy. Bad. So bad. Me so bad.

But Magnus Fin didn't want to hang around in the foul stinking ruin or listen to the regrets of the ghostly eel. He took command.

Right then – the key – we have to do this fast. Where is it? It's got to be somewhere in all this rubble. Where in this heap of stones and junk was the throne?

As they travelled Magnus Fin had snatched up a few strands of kelp. He pressed them now to his nose. Fin turned a quick circle. Piles of stones and junk lay heaped all around. Fin kicked aside a tumbled pillar, and immediately felt sick. The ghost of the conger eel had definitely brought him to the right place. Under the rubble and junk lay picked white bones and skeletons – thousands of them.

The shadowy form of the eel slithered on, over more and more heaps of broken stones until it slinked to a stop. By now they had entered the dark heart of the ruin, which Tarkin would probably call the epicentre! An eerie atmosphere pervaded this place, which was dominated by a tower of rubble. At the foot of the hideous tower, skulls lay embedded in grey sand. Above Fin's head one plastic bottle spun spookily as though caught up in a never-ending whirlpool.

The ghost of the conger had vanished. Fin twisted around, scanning the morbid place for the remains of the great white shark and for a key. Faced with the ruins of a mighty palace the attempt to find a tiny key felt hopeless. To pull back the rubble and search under every fallen stone would take for ever – and his so-called guide seemed to have gone.

Wish I'd never agreed to do his killing. The dry groan jabbed into Fin's brain. *Wish I'd never been born. Here we are – oh how the mighty fall. Like me, the monster king has no rest. Like me he's still around.*

Magnus Fin recoiled, terrified. His foot struck a slumped rock. Instantly he jolted forward and spun round. What did the ghostly eel mean, still around?

Like me he can't let go. Me, I hold on to the awful memories. Him, he holds on to the vain hope that still, somehow, he could be king of the land. What a fool!

Where? Fin found courage. He twisted round slowly in the water. He had fought with the monster king before, and he had won. Now, if he understood the ghostly eel, he was going to have to fight with the monster king again – except this time it would be with his ghost. *Where is he?*

Oh, you can't see him. He's not even a shadow like me. But he's here alright, clinging on. To find the key you'll have to get past him.

Magnus Fin clenched his fists and grasped his moon-stone for courage. If he had to, he would! He kicked back his heels, glided forward and began to circle the great tower of rubble. From out of the corner of his eye he saw the shadow of the eel slither off. Fin swam slower now, sensing the presence of the monster ghost. The murky water trembled. A stone dislodged from the great tower and tumbled in slow motion down, down to the terrible depths.

Where are you? Fin shouted. *Come out and show yourself. It's all over, sad ghost. It's time for King Neptune to rule the seas with wisdom once more.*

Another stone tumbled, this one rolling in Fin's direction, as though pushed by an invisible hand. Fin darted aside. Something was there, he was sure.

It's time to give up. The sea has suffered enough, do you hear me? You have to let go. Your terrible reign is over; you have to understand that.

At that moment the trembling water stilled. Fin, hoping his words had convinced the monster ghost, swam faster now. He was filled with the courage of his moon-stone. There was no time to lose. Would he find the key, glinting and golden, behind this mound of rubble? Magnus Fin pulled back a stone from the heap.

At that very moment the still water thrashed out in a frenzy. Fin was flung back as a solid wall of water crashed over him.

Chapter 25

A stone hurtled through the water. Fin ducked, just in time to feel the force of that stone skim his head.

Where are you? Fin shouted, twisting round. He grabbed a stone from the mound of rubble to shield his face.

The water ahead of him grew darker. Suddenly a spray of bones shot from that darkness. With his stone shield Magnus Fin batted them off. A gasping, choking moan spread through the water. The invading voice seemed to wind round his throat. At the same moment Magnus Fin felt a cold pressure clamp against his arms. The moaning, invisible force shook him. It prised the stone shield from him. Wrenched from his grip the stone fell away, bouncing off in slow motion.

Magnus Fin grasped at the muscular force that was now pinning his arms down. Though there was nothing to see save furious swirling water, something sinister had a hold of him, and it squeezed him with a vice-like grip.

Though the monster ghost was strong and invisible, Magnus Fin had his own human-selkie strength. It pulsed from his heart; it flowed in his blood. He sunk his fingers into the great weight that held him and he pushed. With every ounce of strength he pushed. Astonished, he felt the cold thing slipping away.

It's time to let go, Fin cried, thrusting the quivering weight off him.

Fin's victory was short lived. The sea lashed back, pushing down on his throat. Fighting for breath Fin grabbed at the ghostly force and tried to drive it off. The water pounded him as the ghostly pressure wound tighter and tighter.

An unbearable haunted sigh slithered into his ears. Magnus Fin struggled to block it out but it threatened to drive him mad. In desperation he imagined he could hear Aquella's song, reaching out to him from the land.

With one almighty surge of strength he sunk his fingers into the cold mass and grappled. He heard Aquella sing. He wrestled with the monster ghost. He pushed and he pushed. All the time her song grew louder. Fin felt the ghost weaken. The churning sea grew limp. Pulsing life rushed back into his body. Magnus Fin hurled the thing off, but this time was ready for its return.

It's over, Fin shouted. *This broken palace, this game – it's over. The sea was never yours in the first place. And the treasure is not yours. Let the one who knows how to rule the seas rule them. You've done enough harm. You don't have to live like...*

Fin felt a punch in his back. He swung round. He felt a punch in his stomach. Then in amazement watched as the swirling water in front of him took shape. From the churning murk a huge fish seemed to materialise. It had scales, red glinting scales. It was as big as a man, as slippery as an eel and had no eyes. It was like no fish Fin had ever seen. He reached out with both hands to seize the monstrous fish. The writhing creature squirmed in his hands. Like a mad thing it twisted but Fin held tight. Magnus Fin was strong. He wrestled with the fish, squeezing it tight, till it shrunk. Horrified Fin watched the fish grow smaller and smaller, then slither free, only to return a moment later. But not as a fish.

A dark whirlpool spun. From it long spidery legs emerged. What looked like a Japanese warrior crab lashed out at him and tore a gash in Fin's wetsuit. What was happening? Was this the same invisible force that had threatened to suffocate him?

Fin thrashed out through the water. He kicked. He punched, but the hideous warrior crab, like a boxer, danced and hopped about, first in front then behind, taunting him with its many legs. It scratched him with its sharp pincers.

Wincing, Fin retreated. How could he fight a warrior crab? He scooped up a stone from the rubble and hurled it, smashing two of its legs. The creature toppled forward. Fin fell upon it and tore at its other legs, but in his hands the hard legs turned to grey jelly. The jelly turned to tentacles. Now he was wrestling with a writhing squid.

The jelly tentacles thrashed out, slapping across Magnus Fin's face. It stung, but gone were the killer metallic tentacles the awful creature had had in life. For this was a form Magnus Fin recognised. He had forced the monster ghost to take the shadowy shape of the mutated giant octopus it had been in life.

Fin clung on, pulling at the jelly-like legs. But where Fin only had two arms the ghost had many tentacles. Fin tried to grab two at once, but they squirmed through his fingers like mush.

Fin wrestled, pushing and punching into the blob. The clammy substance stuck to his face, threatening to suffocate him. He shoved it off, but instantly felt the cold tentacles wrap round his legs. He yanked them off and dug his elbow hard into the sticky mass, sending the ghost-creature lurching backwards.

In the next second the grey, repulsive bulk surged forward. The sea churned. The phantom bloated. It was hard to tell what was water, what was ghost. Fin sharpened his eye-lights then pounced on the shuddering blob. Though no more than thrashing jelly, the fiend wasn't defeated yet. Fin shook it. He squeezed and crushed it. Strength he didn't know he possessed burned in him. Under his hands he felt the slime grow limp. He was winning. He was sure of that.

It's over, Fin shouted. *It's time to finally let go, do you hear me?*

With a colossal shove he pushed the creature off him. As the glue-like form oozed away Fin felt something hard scrape across his hand. Fin grabbed at it. It was a claw, clenched and hard as metal. Then his probing hand brushed over something else. Something soft. Something dark.

With both hands Fin grabbed at the clenched claw and shook it. What was it holding? Whatever it was, the spectre of the monster king was clutching on to it with every last ounce of ghostly strength.

Fin pulled at the claw. He felt it judder. The sea sloshed about them, but Fin strove to force the claw apart. All the sea ghost's power went into grasping hold of this soft, dark thing. But what was it? Fin felt it brush over his hand again. Whatever it was felt strangely familiar.

The monster ghost groaned and its claw thrashed the water, hurling Magnus Fin backwards. He crashed back against a shark's skull and watched, horrified, as the ghost reformed all of its grey ghostly tentacles and lashed them through the dank water like whips. But its one claw still clutched the dark thing.

Fin dived forward, wrapped his arms around a frenzied tentacle and hung on tight. As the monster ghost thrashed him downwards, to smash him against rocks, Fin dived free and grasped the clutching claw.

Magnus Fin wouldn't be shaken off again. The creature was raving mad now. Incensed, it pulsed and convulsed, hurling debris everywhere. Rubble, like missiles, careered towards Fin. He ducked but clung on, plunging his nails into the claw. To give him strength, he imagined Aquella singing. It drowned out the awful sighing. Her song grew louder. Fin forced the claw open. Hope leapt in him as he felt the creature grow limp. The ghost was beaten; he knew it.

Wrenching the claw apart Magnus Fin tugged at the thing it had so desperately clung on to. He gasped. It was fur, and not just any fur. The ghost was clinging to a seal skin.

Feeling the softness of the fur, his heart raced. Could it be? Could it possibly be? The fur felt warm and thick and good. Fin elbowed away the remnants of the quivering creature. Its strength was spent. Carefully Magnus Fin tugged at the fur till finally it slipped free from the awful claw. Hope burned in him. Could this possibly be Aquella's seal skin?

Magnus Fin pressed the dark pelt to him, and at the same moment he felt the sea ghost tremble and withdraw.

You can go now, Fin shouted. *There's nothing to cling on to any more. You can be something better, something wiser.*

The water shuddered. The grey jelly-like ghost shrunk, and shrunk. The sea quivered then grew still. Magnus Fin stared in astonishment as the ghost took the shape of a small bright blue fish. The awful sighing was gone. The terrible greed, Fin knew, was gone.

Magnus Fin, pressing the seal skin to his chest, looked in wonder as the small creature flicked its tail and swam off. It had been released. Somehow Fin understood, it would harm no more.

With a lump in his throat he pressed the dark fur to his face and breathed it in. He couldn't believe it! He had found Aquella's seal skin! By some magic, the seal skin was whole again, not torn to shreds as Aquella believed. It was perfect.

Well done. You fought well. You won.

Fin swung round. The shadowy conger eel swam towards him.

I have not been released as he has. But perhaps my turn will come. Now I can show you the broken throne. Come.

Yes, we have to hurry, said Fin. *I can feel the current changing. Neptune's brewing another storm. Quick, show me where to find the key.*

Chapter 26

Magnus Fin squeezed Aquella's seal skin inside his wetsuit and glided through the murk. He felt exhausted after the ghostly wrestle but also exhilarated after the victory. But this was no time for glory. The task was not yet complete. The precious Seudan waited in the unopened kist in the cave. The key was not yet found. Fin slowed down as the ghost of the conger eel swayed back and forth in front of yet another heap of rubble.

Where have you brought me? Fin called to it. *Is this where the banqueting hall was?*

Yes. Under this rubble. Under these fallen walls and pillars. But you'll never find your key, came the mournful voice, *and I am useless. Insubstantial spectre that I am.*

Fin kicked back his heels and approached the pile of rubble. Nothing in this ruin resembled the mighty glittering palace that had once stood on the ocean floor. Fin circled the heap of stones. *Are you sure?*

It doesn't look like it, I know. But this was the banqueting hall. Trust me.

Fin gazed for a moment at the sad ghost. *I trust you,* he said, then reached out and grabbed at loose stones.

The stones were heavy and to dislodge just one took great effort. Fin groaned. There were perhaps five thousand stones piled up. How would he ever find the key? Aquella had said the great white shark guarded the monster's keys, and the great white shark had been crushed in the banqueting hall moments before the whole palace came crashing down. So Magnus Fin was going to have to pull back all these stones until he got to the bottom. It seemed impossible!

He managed to push back ten, twenty, thirty, forty stones. Already his arms were aching. It had been easier to wrestle with the ghost of the monster king. He dislodged another, then another – but thousands still remained. Magnus Fin kept going. Some stones were small, others were huge. He struggled with an enormous stone, scraped his fingers, broke his nails. Finally he succeeded in toppling the mighty stone then sank back, resting his aching limbs as he watched the stone tumble through the water. It rolled and bounced. He watched it veer off into the gloom, then gaped in amazement as several silvery glittering shapes came gliding out of that same gloom and swam towards him.

That's him!

Yeah, pal, you're the greatest!

The champ!

Anything we can do for you, bro. Just give us the nod. Cos we just cruising.

Just loafing.

Just killing time.

Magnus Fin couldn't believe it. It was the fish gang he had met on his last mission, but what a change.

H-h-hi, he stammered. *How are you all doing? You – you look great!*

We are great! Thanks to you, buddy, thanks to you.

Fin couldn't believe the transformation. What had happened to the ugly, ragged, skinny bunch of fish? The fish that now surrounded him, staring at him with their round glittering eyes were fat and healthy looking. Sure, they still had a few rusting hooks hanging from their lips, trailing strands of seaweed and whatever else they had picked up along the way, but there was a shine to their eyes and they looked happy.

Fin glanced at the shadow of the conger eel that was now slinking around the base of the rubble heap. *Did you have something to do with this?* he asked.

Thought you could do with a bit of help, the ghost of the conger said, sounding, Fin was sure, slightly less depressed than usual.

Relieved, Fin grinned and turned back to the fish gang, who, he realised, couldn't see the slinking shadow of the conger.

We're doing fine, as you can see. Thanks to the feasts you give us, bro. You are the best.

The champ.

The greatest.

Before they repeated their praise Fin interrupted, *Glad you like crusts of old bread.*

Like? They all sang. *Like? Man, we love, we adore, we esteem!*

Fin was impressed with their vocabulary. Not only were their bodies healthier, their conversation was too!

That's great. Mum was throwing it out for the birds, so I thought, you know, might as well chuck it in the sea and feed you.

The fish nodded eagerly. They gazed at Magnus Fin as though he was a god. And Fin gazed at them and their glinting fishing hooks. Then he looked at the mound of rubble, then back at the fish gang.

You might wonder what I'm doing here, Fin said, smiling.

No, bro, we just got the idea to come cruising in this mean-looking place.

Man it's bad.

It's evil, bro.

Yeah, it's the pits. We just found ourselves drifting this way. No reason, no...

Look, interrupted Fin, *King Neptune needs helps – quickly. Me too. If you could help, I'd be really grateful. There's a key buried in there. I'll tell you the whole story later. Just trust me on this one. The great white shark had a set of keys, and he got trapped under the throne when the palace collapsed.* Fin pointed to the heap of rubble. *Maybe you'd be able to squirm in amongst this junk, find the bones and hook the keys up with one of your hooks?*

The fish gang nodded eagerly and swam closer to their hero. They would do anything for this human who stood at the water's edge throwing them food.

Sure thing, bro.

Love to.

Can't wait.

Just say the word.

Nothing we like better than a dangerous adventure.

Lead us on, said Spike, the broken-toothed gang leader. *We're right in front of you!*

The shadowy form of the conger eel slunk around the base of the rubble and nodded its spectral head at a particular stone. Fin sunk down to this stone and poked his fingers under it, trying to make a tiny hole for the fish to squirm through. *I think the shark went this way,* he said.

The fish gang gazed at the chink amongst the pile of bones, skulls and broken stones. Even Spike, who had been in more scrapes than he could remember, drew back and twitched.

Not pretty, he said.

Pretty ugly, said another.

Yeah, I know, but we don't have long. Fin was anxious now that the fish gang might change their minds and swim off. *Listen, guys, I can already feel the current picking up. Neptune's going to make another storm. We have to act fast.* The fish gang had stopped eagerly nodding. *You still want to help?*

Spike nodded, the sign for his gang to nod too. *Key, eh?* he asked, staring at the tiny gap Fin had made between a huge stone and a bone.

Aye, that's right. A key. King Neptune's key.

Five festering hooks hung from Spike's mouth. They had pained him for so long but at last it seemed they would serve him. This tough fish that had got away so many times was ready to help the great King Neptune. He nodded solemnly. *Consider it done,* he said proudly.

With that Spike flicked his tail and called his gang of determined fish who had tugged free from fisherman's lines. The dinner plate was not their fate; adventure was. *Forward,* ordered Spike and like an army they advanced.

As the fish vanished, slithering amongst the ruins of the crumbled throne, Magnus Fin could only tread water and watch them go.

And that's when the tide turned.

Chapter 27

Far out at sea, towering waves buffeted a small yacht. It pitched into the wind and looked as though it would be swallowed up by the angry sea.

The yacht wasn't the only thing being battered by the storm. Ahead of it a beautiful mermaid struggled against the pounding waves. Her long dark hair flew back in the tempest. Her turquoise tail flashed as she was flung up then down. But she, like the selkies, knew the power and magic in song. Though the salt spray lashed over her face and the swell threatened to drive her off course, she sang to still the storm. She sang to guide the yacht. She sang to summon the land.

Eastwards she swam, the whole ocean now stirred to a thrashing fury. Waves reared high then came crashing down. Wild white horses of spume galloped over the Atlantic Ocean. Frantically the mermaid glanced over her shoulder. The brave yacht rode the mighty waves. It wouldn't be another wreck festering at the bottom of the sea. Exhausted she kept going. With the last of her strength she sang.

While deep under the sea the swell grew, and grew.

Magnus Fin turned frantic circles with his arms. He felt the strong current suck him away from the pile of rubble. Fighting against the storm's force he swam back.

The fish gang hadn't returned. They'd been in there for ages. Where were they?

Hurry! he shouted. *Hurry, the tide is turning. The ruins will be sucked under the sands. You have to come out. You'll be buried alive. Hurry! Neptune's whipping up a storm.*

Magnus Fin looked anxiously round for the ghost of the conger eel. Would the powerful swell of the sea mean anything to a ghost?

Fin had never felt so alone. Below him the sands trembled. The tidal waters dragged and sloshed. Fin grabbed hold of a slumped pillar and clung to it, to stop the swell hurling him against the rubble. The angry tide heaved and rushed now, lashing at rocks, hurling boulders, flinging bones. Any moment the throne heap would be swallowed up. Still Fin clung to the pillar. He couldn't peel his gaze away from the place the fish had vanished into.

Please, storm, hold back just another minute. Please, he cried, *please!*

It's done.

Fin swung round. The slinking shape of the conger ghost slithered over the ocean floor. Fin heard a deep sigh tremble through its voice. *I'm going home now.*

We got it, bro, took a while, but we found it!

Real nasty in there.

That was one smashed-up great white!

Dangling from Spike's largest hook was a bunch of keys!

Took some finding, Spike went on. *Some evil mess in there. Oh, bro, you don't want to know! Gross!*

Swim! Magnus Fin shouted as the mighty sea swell rushed over the rubble, flinging stones and hurling bones. *We have to get out of here. Quick!*

The fish gang, as one, turned and darted off. Magnus Fin followed. The heaving sea battered them and carried them away from the ruins. The churning waters flung them far from the gloom and destruction. There was no resisting the force of the sea now. Mighty tidal waves reared high, and like champion surfers they rode the waves.

The first pink light streaked the eastern sky when a wave threw Magnus Fin, spluttering and gasping, above the surface. In the distance he could see the cliffs and beach of home. But where was the fish gang? The sea had grown strangely calm now. Fin lowered himself back under the water then plunged deep. As he dived he scanned the surrounding sea with his torchlights.

That wave had to be a hundred metres high at least! Man, that was a blast!

Fin swung round. It was Spike, with the keys still dangling from his hook. *Where did you go, bro? We dig nothing better than riding the surf. Wow, I must have leapt as high as the clouds.*

High as the moon.

High as the sun. That's what I call fun!

The other members of the fish gang appeared, looking like they'd just survived twenty goes on the high-speed big dipper at the funfair.

Relief tingled through Fin's exhausted body. He scanned the water, wondering what had become of the conger eel. In the back of his mind he heard the ghost's voice almost happy now: *I'm going home!*

Thanks! Fin called to him, wherever he was. *And good luck!*

Now it was the hum of the sea and the jangling of fish-hooks that Fin could hear. And something else far in the distance – the faint and beautiful sound of Aquella singing.

Magnus Fin pulled out the hidden seal skin and flapped it out in the clear water, cleaning it. Exhaustion fled and he felt strong again. Then, like a streak of black and orange lightning, he led the fish gang into the bay. As he swam, the precious shining black seal skin, like a flag of victory, wafted free.

Chapter 28

On the sandy beach dawn was breaking. Fulmars were up, preening themselves on their craggy ledges, chattering loudly. Aquella sang. Sometimes the fulmars stopped chattering, cocked their white heads and seemed to listen. Her song drifted out over the stormy sea while, unopened in the cave behind her, lay the rusty kist.

With her eyes closed Aquella sang, so she didn't see Magnus Fin hoist himself up to the high black rock and shake the salt water from his hair.

Magnus Fin jumped over the rocks. In his wetsuit pocket he had the keys. Hidden behind his back he clasped the seal skin. Twice he stopped and waved in Aquella's direction but she didn't wave back. Her song rippled clear and strong. Even the tough fish gang, as Magnus Fin unhooked the precious keys from Spike's fish-hook, had wept to hear her singing. Spike had told Fin, *We wear our hearts on our scales, bro. We such emotional fish.*

Magnus Fin walked steadily now, over the stony beach and onto the stretch of soft sand. The strength of the land seeped into him. Drawing closer he saw that Aquella had her eyes closed. He shook out her seal skin in the early morning breeze. Still Aquella sang, though Fin detected her nostrils quiver.

Fin padded over the sand towards her. Without a sound he knelt down next to her. He held the seal skin in both hands and as gently as he could placed it on her lap. Aquella's song didn't falter. Her nostrils widened as she bent her head and sniffed the air. Her quivering fingers found the pelt. She kept singing. Tears ran down her face. She dug her fingers into the fur. Still she kept singing. She took up her seal coat and pressed it to her chest. She kept singing, though now you couldn't tell what was sobbing and what was song.

"My seal skin," she cried finally, tears spilling down her face. "My very own seal skin. I've got it back at last." She buried her face in the warm, clean, perfect fur.

Tarkin had hardly slept a wink. By the sound of his mother pacing around and sighing loudly all night long, it seemed she'd hardly slept either. It was early morning when the smell of pancakes and maple syrup wafted up from the kitchen. Tarkin pushed open the kitchen door. It was only seven a.m. What, he wondered, was his mother doing having pancakes at seven a.m.? As he stepped into the warm kitchen his mother, who was sitting at the table, looked up at him, and wearily shook her head. "I worry about you sometimes, Tarkin. I really do."

"But, Mom, you asked for the truth. It's the truth." He slipped into his usual seat at the table, and fiddled with his shark's tooth necklace. The night before he'd told her the whole story – about the sighting of the mermaid, and the selkies, and the scary teenager. "Seriously, Mom, I'm not making it up!"

"So basically," his mother said, "you threw my mother's precious pearl necklace into the sea?" She drizzled maple syrup on a pancake.

"But it wasn't like that. I hoped she would see it and come out of the water. Then I dropped it by mistake."

For a while no one said anything. Martha bit off an end of pancake and chewed loudly. "Oh, Tarkin, you act like you're three or something. You act like these kids with imaginary friends. You make me uncomfortable when you talk that way."

"Well, it's true."

"I know what's true. I had a precious necklace belonging to my dear mother, and now I don't. That's what's true."

"I'll try and get it back." Tarkin touched his mother gently on the arm. "Can I have a pancake?"

She laughed then, a tired hopeless laugh. "Sure you can. But listen to me: don't do anything foolish. Losing the necklace is bad enough. I don't want to lose you too!" Then she smiled at him, got up and spooned batter into the frying pan. Tarkin knew he was forgiven, but even so, he still felt bad.

"I'm really sorry, Mom."

At that moment they heard the familiar thud of letters being dropped through the letterbox. Tarkin jumped to his feet, like he always did, and ran through to the hallway. He came back with a bundle of leaflets about supermarket deals and who to vote for at the next election. There was nothing from his dad.

His mother caught his look of disappointment and said quickly, "I got pizza in for lunch. Your favourite."

"Great," Tarkin said without enthusiasm. He hadn't even eaten breakfast yet. He didn't have the appetite to think about lunch. But nonetheless he tried to push the familiar disappointment away as he dropped the flyers into the bin. He looked up, and managed a weak smile. "With pepperoni and mozzarella?"

His mother nodded and scooped the hot pancake onto a plate. For the time being, it seemed, the missing necklace was forgotten. But for Tarkin it wasn't so easy to forget the other missing thing in his life – his dad. For the hundredth time he wondered, *Where is he? Why hasn't he written?*

His mother pushed the bottle of maple syrup across the table. "Want some?"

Tarkin nodded. Then he rolled the sweet pancake, picked it up and bit into it. He licked syrup from his chin and eyed the kitchen clock. It was twenty past seven, and it wasn't even a school day. He finished his pancake, kissed his mother on the cheek and went out into the bright June morning. With any luck he might catch Magnus Fin doing a spot of beachcombing, or treasure hunting. Or maybe he'd found the key! Maybe he was going to open the box?

Tarkin sprinted down the hillside and over the bridge. Running fast helped him forget his worries. Soon it was excitement fluttering inside him as he sped along the beach path. That was the thing about having a friend like Magnus Fin; you never knew just what he might be up to. For all Tarkin knew, his best friend might be having breakfast with the great King Neptune himself.

Tarkin was out of breath by the time he reached the beach. In the distance, close to the cave, he saw two figures sitting on the sand. "Fin!" he yelled, then whooped three times – that was their signal. He saw Fin raise a hand and wave back. It looked like Aquella sitting beside him. Tarkin ran towards them, his ponytail flapping in the breeze.

But Tarkin wasn't the only one that Saturday morning who had risen early and set off for the beach.

Billy Mole hadn't slept a wink either. Something fishy was going on. It frightened Billy. It gave him the creeps, but in another way it fascinated him. He'd never encountered anything like this in his whole seventeen years. He'd stumbled upon some kind of mystery, and now for the life of him he didn't know what to do about it. Billy Mole got up, put on his now crumpled clothes and went out into the bright morning. His heart thumped. His mind boggled. He turned his steps in the direction of the beach.

Chapter 29

Tarkin, long legs leaping over the sand and stones, made it to the cave in seconds, whooping, yelling scuffing up sand and forgetting all about Mission Act Normal. He didn't notice the black fur that Aquella had stuffed inside her green jacket, even though bits stuck out. His eyes fell instead to the bunch of keys in Magnus Fin's hand.

"Wow!" Tarkin exclaimed, thumping Fin on the arm. "You did it! You're so awesome. You..."

Fin shook his head. "It wasn't just me. I've got a few friends out there." Fin nodded in the direction of the ocean. "They found them. All I did was promise to throw them some sausage rolls."

Tarkin wasn't too interested in the details. "So – come on, come on – aren't you gonna open the box? I had a hunch, you know? I'm never up this early, but something told me, 'Tark, get yourself down there. Quick!'" Tarkin grinned, nodded and gestured towards the cave.

"I had a hunch you'd turn up too," said Fin. "That's why we hung on. Aquella and I have been here for ages waiting for you."

It was Tarkin who reached the mouth of the cave first. He found the precious box hidden under its camouflage of seaweed and stared down at the pongy mess plonked higgledy-piggledy over it. His eyes fell to the footsteps in the sand beside the box. He looked worried and turned to Fin and Aquella who had just reached the mouth of the cave. "I get the feeling someone's been here."

Fin flashed a look back along the beach. "It's OK, Tark," he said, stepping into the cave and kneeling down beside the kist. "No one's opened it. That's the main thing." He would tell Tarkin all about the snooping teenager, but not now. Now was the time to see if one of these keys fitted the kist, discover what was inside and, if it was Neptune's stolen treasure, return it to him.

Tarkin hopped from foot to foot. "Man, I'm so glad I came along."

"Me too," added Aquella, fishing a hankie from her pocket. "Don't touch the kist, Fin. Here," she handed him a clump of dried kelp, "use this as a kind of glove."

Tarkin and Aquella stood on either side, while Magnus Fin, down on his knees level with the kist, wrapped the kelp around his hand. With his covered hand he swept away the seaweed then stroked the kist. He tapped it. He patted the rough surface and after what seemed like for ever he found the small keyhole.

With shaking hands he found the small silver key that looked as if it would fit the lock. "I've – I've got it," he whispered, his voice trembling with anticipation.

"Does it fit? Oh boy, come on, Fin, turn the key." Tarkin peered over Fin's shoulder. So did Aquella.

With quivering fingers Magnus Fin fitted the small silver key into the keyhole.

For what seemed an eternity all three were silent, hearts thudding, pulses racing, wide eyes staring. Then out of the unbearable silence came the crunching sound of a key turning in a lock.

Aquella gasped, Tarkin let out a squeal of joy and Magnus Fin trembled as he opened the lid of the rusty old kist.

Their silence while the key turned in the lock was nothing compared to their silence when the lid was opened. Vivid light streamed out, so intense they all staggered back and covered their eyes. Tarkin wanted to yell and cheer but kept his mouth shut. This was Fin's moment. But words escaped Magnus Fin. Awe-struck he could only tremble and shield his eyes. His jaw fell open. Never in his life had he seen anything so dazzling: jewels so bright he could hardly look at them. It was like the sun and all the planets glowing in the box.

"It's... it's... " He swallowed hard and tried again. "It's real treasure!" His voice wobbled with emotion. "It really is! It's the Seudan!"

"The *Seudan*," murmured Aquella, "the jewels of the ocean."

Shimmering jewels, as radiant as the box was ugly, lay nestled one against the other. And they weren't the kind of jewels normally seen by humans. Each precious jewel shone like the sun blazing down on a miniature ocean, glistening red, white, purple, emerald and gold.

For a while Magnus Fin, Tarkin and Aquella, pressed back against the wall of the cave, could only shield their eyes and gasp. But after some moments, the intense light, which at first was blinding, grew warm and soft until the jewels in the kist seemed to glow kindly. They took hesitant steps forward then Tarkin and Aquella paused. It was only right that Magnus Fin should be the first to step up to the kist.

In awe Magnus Fin gazed down, his heart pounding. With shaking hands, and this time with no kelp to protect him, he knelt down and lifted a golden ball from the kist. The golden ball shone like the sun. As he held it he felt great love and strength pour into him. As he lifted it to his ear he could hear the deep rippling, booming music of the ocean. And his heart glowed. Symbols, he saw, were etched onto this stone, ancient and mysterious. These symbols, Magnus Fin understood, contained instructions on ruling the sea. With the Seudan in safe hands, wisdom would never be forgotten. Here was wave-making, sea-cleaning, swells and rip curls, high tides and low. With trembling hands Magnus Fin studied the symbols.

He returned the golden ball to the kist then looked up at Tarkin, whose eyes sparkled with light from the precious jewels. "Hold one," Fin murmured.

"Yes," whispered Aquella, who ventured forward and stroked the jewels. "And wish on it. There are garnets, jasper, quartz, emerald, amethyst and gold." She closed her eyes and made a wish.

Fin and Tarkin gazed at Aquella, astonished she knew the names of the precious jewels. Taking a deep breath Tarkin reached into the kist and lifted out a deep purple gem, craggy and sparkling.

"That's amethyst," Aquella declared.

Tarkin gazed at the amethyst, carved as it was with the script of the sea. He pressed it against his cheek, closed his eyes and wished. While he did Aquella took a step back, then another. Noiselessly she slipped away.

Tarkin opened his eyes when he heard a yelp in the distance, followed by a splash. He returned the purple jewel to the kist and looked anxiously around. "Where's Aquella?"

"She's gone," Fin replied. "Back to the sea. That was probably her wish."

Tarkin's gaze landed on the green puffy jacket that lay on the sand by the mouth of the cave. Beside it lay her hat and her pink scarf. He couldn't believe it; Aquella had returned to the sea!

Chapter 30

Standing in the cave with the brilliant shining Seudan between them, a shadow of anxiety darkened Tarkin's face. "And what was your wish, Fin?" he asked, imagining that Magnus Fin might also slip into the sea, leaving him, who couldn't even swim, standing on the beach alone.

"You really want me to tell you?" Fin asked.

Tarkin nodded and sunk to his knees. He felt a lump rise in his throat.

"That the selkies return to the bay. That there's always a place for magic and for people who are a bit different. That's there's always clean water, birds, fish. That there's a place for everyone and everything... do you want me to carry on?"

"But you won't go, Fin, will you?"

Magnus Fin smiled at him, his brown eye deep and warm, his green eye shining. "I've got a foot in both worlds, you know that, Tark. I'll go and I'll come back. But if all these newspapers and TV cameras came after me, then I don't know what I'd do. Maybe then I'd have to go. Maybe you would too."

At that moment came the sound of pebbles crunching behind them. Magnus Fin and Tarkin spun round and jumped to their feet, jostling together, trying to block the treasure chest from the snooping teenager who stood at the mouth of the cave. He said nothing but just stood there, framed black against the dazzling brightness.

"What do you want?" Fin asked, his voice calm and steady.

"Yeah," said Tarkin, "like, what you doing here?"

Billy Mole wouldn't make eye contact. He kept his head down and took an awkward shuffled step into the cave, coughing nervously. Gone was his swagger, his cocky confidence. Looking at his feet he said, "Was it you?"

Tarkin looked confused but not Magnus Fin. "And if it was?" Any fear he'd felt for this teenager was gone. He felt angry. How dare he come snooping around? It was because of him the selkies were miles away in Sule Skerrie. Fin took a step towards him, caring not that he, who was not even twelve years old, was standing up to a boy of at least sixteen. "What would you do? Tell the world? Write in your magazine that in the far north of Scotland there is still a little bit of magic left? Then what? Send in your cameras, your film-makers and wipe us out?"

Tarkin kept quiet, but nodded vigorously along with everything Fin said.

"Remember the girl you chased?" Magnus Fin continued.

Billy Mole nodded but still kept his eyes glued to his scuffed black shoes.

"Well, you might want to know – she's gone. And half my family are gone. Are you happy now? Is that what you wanted? Get rid of the ones that are different. Make us all the same. Was that your plan?"

Billy Mole shook his head, sniffed loudly and wiped his nose with his sleeve. "No, n-no," he stuttered, "no...

I..." Words failed him. But he wasn't happy; that much was clear. He stretched out his hand towards Magnus Fin – the hand that had been cut and swollen.

"You – it was you made it better, wasn't it?" Then he dared to raise his head. From where he stood it seemed as though Magnus Fin glowed. He glimpsed the moon-stone around Magnus Fin's neck. He saw his mismatched eyes. "It was you!" His jaw fell open. His whole body shook like a leaf. He shielded his eyes from the glare.

"Yes, it was me," Fin said.

"Th-thanks," stammered Billy.

Tarkin gazed from one to the other as though he was at a tennis match.

"How did you do it?"

"That's Neptune's business," said Fin, then he took another step forward. As he did he revealed the treasure chest behind him. Billy gasped at the flood of brilliant light. He dropped his hand and his eyes fell upon the glittering jewels. "And that," added Fin sharply, "is King Neptune's treasure."

Stunned, Billy Mole, half covering his eyes, peered at the bright jewels. The glow from the jewels warmed him. He stopped shaking. Maybe he understood that this treasure was not about money and fame. Maybe he understood that each shining jewel was a clean ocean, a good wind, a mighty whale, a healthy salmon. Into his bewildered thoughts he heard Magnus Fin say to him, *Let us live in peace; that's all we want.*

Billy flushed red. Words failed him. He hung his head.

"Yeah," added Tarkin, "don't write about things you don't understand."

An awkward silence hung between them, then Billy, his voice so small and so changed from the "Oi! Fish boy!" one, said, "I don't understand all this stuff. It's weird. I just wanted to get on. You know, do a good job. Honest. Like, they sent me up here. 'You're gonna hit the big time, Billy boy,' that's what they said." Billy Mole twisted his hands together.

"Looks like you have," Tarkin said.

"But this 'big time' is a secret," Fin said. "Some things are not for everyone to know. This is one of them. Magic does exist. At least up here it does. You stumbled into that secret, and I'm asking you to keep it." Magnus Fin looked at him, willing him to lift his head.

As if by hypnosis Billy Mole looked up. Magnus Fin, who seemed to be on fire with the dazzling light, stared at him. As he stared he saw Billy Mole's eyes soften. He saw a light go on in those eyes. Then Magnus Fin nodded, and looked away.

Billy coughed like he might choke. He rubbed his eyes. He brought his hand over his heart. "It's like, in here, I understand you folks... your magic." He rubbed his eyes again. "I never seen anything so bright! Maybe I believed in magic once. But I forgot. Dunno why. It's like a light goes out. But you – you've still got it."

"That's right," said Magnus Fin, smiling now at this teenager who looked on the verge of tears. "We've still got it. But you know what, maybe you have too..." Then Magnus Fin gestured to the kist of riches. "Why don't you hold one of the precious stones? They're magic, you know. You could make a wish."

As if in a trance Billy Mole stepped forwards, bent down and lifted out a round emerald stone. For a long while he held it. A bright fat tear that looked like a gem slid down his face.

"I don't know what happened," he sobbed. "Maybe I grew up." He wiped his tears on the sleeve of his jacket and sniffed loudly. "But it's, like, still inside me. Just cos you get older, you don't have to lose the magic, do you?" Then for the first time in a long time a smile lit up his face.

In the selkie thought-speak Magnus Fin called out to Aquella, *The one who was after us – he'll keep the secret. I'm sure of that now. Tell the others. Tell them to come home.*

Tarkin, accustomed now to the vivid light, poured over the Seudan, trying to decipher the symbols on the stones. They were like hieroglyphs, like picture writing.

Fin stepped towards the kist and murmured, as much to himself as to anyone, "I have to return the Seudan to Neptune." He grasped his own moon-stone, which was, he realised, like a tiny nugget of the Seudan. No wonder it protected him. Magnus Fin hoped it would guide him on this last task – to find Neptune's cavern and return the stolen treasure. All he had to do was wait for Miranda's signal.

A few moments later a noise of rolling pebbles reached their ears. Fin ran to the mouth of the cave in time to see a beautiful black seal slither and bounce over the stones. She hauled herself up to him, yelped then nuzzled Fin's leg with her nose.

"It's Aquella," shouted Tarkin, running to pat her.

Billy Mole placed the emerald stone back in the box, stumbled to the mouth of the cave and gazed at the seal. Words failed him. It was enough to stare – at a seal called Aquella and at a boy with different coloured eyes who, Billy was certain, had only last night been a seal himself. Billy couldn't write this story even if he wanted to. No one would believe him. He could only shake his head in amazement. Meanwhile Aquella raised her beautiful head and clapped her flippers together.

Magnus Fin turned and grinned at Billy Mole. "She's come back," he said, his face breaking into a huge smile.

Chapter 31

They spent a long time on the beach that morning. Fin and Tarkin showed Billy Mole how to prize periwinkles off stones, and how to scramble over rocks, and how to jump over waves and make a rock pool full of sea anemones, jellyfish and crabs.

While the boys were busy leaping over rocks, Aquella took off her precious seal skin. She found a secret place in the cave, rolled it up and hid it. By this time the sun was warm and there was no need for her puffy jacket or hat and scarf. Wearing her T-shirt and jeans she ran down to the rocks. Now it didn't matter about salt water; she had a seal skin. Now she could live freely in both worlds, as a girl on the land and a selkie in the sea.

She told them about the solstice celebrations. Fin didn't ask how she knew, as selkie time moved differently. He guessed Aquella had been all the way to Sule Skerrie.

"And you can come to the party, too, if you like," she said, turning to Billy Mole.

Billy hadn't been invited to a party for a long time. "You serious? I mean, yeah, ace, I'd love to." He rubbed his hands together. Then he stopped. "You, um, won't catch me with a fishing line, will you?"

Aquella laughed and winked. "If you behave yourself I won't."

Billy looked relieved. Tarkin laughed and Fin cheered. Then Aquella told them about the wedding. How it would be an extra special solstice party this year because her brother Ronan and her best friend Lorelie were getting married. "And I've to be the selkie bridesmaid," she added, tossing back her long black hair and twirling around.

"That's great," Fin laughed, congratulating her. Then he glanced out to sea. "Where are they?" he asked, turning back to Aquella.

"They should be on their way back to the bay. Can't you see them?"

Sure enough, the still water frothed as one by one sleek seal heads rose from the water. Lively yelps sounded from the bay. Then Miranda lifted her head from the water and called to the shore. Fin waved wildly, then turned to their new friend from London.

"That's my grandmother," he explained, pointing to the silvery shape in the midst of the seals. "Can you see her? The big silver one. She's queen of the selkies."

"You telling me your grandmother is a seal?" Billy asked, but the scorn was gone from his voice. He smiled then, and waved to Magnus Fin's grandmother in the sea. "She's ace!" he said. And there was something about the tone of his voice and the changed expression on his face that told Magnus Fin he meant it.

Fin, Tarkin, Aquella and Billy all stood on the skerries, whooping, calling out and waving to the seals. But it was only Magnus Fin – the expert beachcomber – who spied the wooden crate washed in with the tide.

For Neptune's treasures, Miranda said, then flicked back her tail fins and vanished under the sea.

This was the sign.

Now it was time to go.

"Fin! Magnus Fin!"

Fin glanced back over his shoulder, then lifted his arm and waved. "It's Dad," he yelled, and leapt over the rock pool, jumped down off the rocks and ran along the beach towards him. As he approached he saw his dad's expression. He was beaming from ear to ear and gesturing excitedly.

"Son," he called, "Mum's cooking sausages for breakfast. Tell Aquella and bring Tarkin if you want. We've got some good news."

Fin slowed, and felt a sick feeling lurch the pit of his stomach. *Good news!* He knew all about the good news. He bit his lip and looked down. He couldn't bear to burst his parents' bubble. He opened his mouth but no words came. Ragnor, though, didn't seem aware of his son's awkwardness.

"Aye, great news. We've won something, but I'm not saying what. Mum wants to break it to you herself. We thought you'd be down here treasure hunting." Ragnor looked into the distance. "Hey! Quite a party you've got this morning." It was only then Ragnor noticed the older boy. "Who's the tall one with the short hair?" he asked. "Don't think I've seen him before."

Magnus Fin would have explained, but he was saved by Aquella who flung her arms wide and fell into her uncle's arms. "I've got it back," she cried. "I've got my seal skin back."

Ragnor hugged her tightly. Fin felt a lump rise in his throat. How, he wondered, did his father feel about Aquella's news? Ragnor was one selkie who would never get his seal skin back. But when Ragnor stepped back his expression was nothing but happiness for Aquella.

"It's all great news today," Ragnor said, beaming. "And it looks like we selkies might have ourselves a wonderful land holi—!" He cupped his hand over his mouth. "Oops! Forget I said that. Come on, it's breakfast time!"

By this time Tarkin and Billy were jumping over the rocks and hurrying towards the others. Magnus Fin took a deep breath. He felt the strength of the golden ball as if the radiant sun was right inside him. He looked at Aquella then at his dad.

"Dad, you were right about the treasure hunting. I need Aquella to help me return Neptune's stolen treasure. I did it; I found the key to the kist in the ruins of the monster's palace. That's where I found Aquella's seal skin. Take Tarkin and Billy home for breakfast. We'll come later. Billy is up here visiting. He's from London. He'll – um – tell you all about the good news."

Ragnor was dumbstruck by his son's achievements.

"Trust us, Uncle Ragnor," Aquella said, squeezing his hand.

"Don't I always? Be brave, young ones," Ragnor replied.

With that Magnus Fin and Aquella dashed down to the shore. It was Magnus Fin who pulled the wooden crate from the tideline and dragged it up to the cave. It was just the right size to hold the kist. The words FINE TEAS FROM INDIA were inscribed in faded lettering on the side of the crate.

By the time a black seal and a boy in a tight wetsuit with a rip in the sleeve, balancing a heavy wooden crate between them, entered the ocean, Ragnor, Tarkin and Billy Mole were making their way up the garden path, the aroma of pork sausages filling the air.

This time it was apologies Billy Mole was practising in his head. Ragnor noticed his reluctance as he stood before the front door, biting his nails. "Come on in, Billy. What's wrong? Don't London lads like Scottish sausages then?"

Barbara was in the middle of lighting a candle when they all stepped into the kitchen. She smiled, recognising the prize giver, then stood back to reveal the feast she'd prepared. "And when we're in sunny Spain," she announced, "we'll eat sausages and paella, and we'll dance flamenco and..."

"Stop. Please stop."

Barbara blew out the match and gave Billy Mole a quizzical look.

Chapter 32

Aquella balanced the crate on her back while Magnus Fin swam alongside, holding on to the crate to keep it steady. They had tried a few different transportation methods, but that way seemed the best. Though the treasure chest was heavy it lost half of its weight under the water, and though it pressed down on Aquella's back it was a pain she could bear.

Magnus Fin had been to Neptune's cavern once before. Miranda had taken him there. Aquella had never been, and the thought of meeting the great king of the sea filled her with awe. Neptune's storm of earlier had died down and the sea was back to its slack and listless mood. With every stroke Fin imagined clean seas, good tides, healthy fish.

Over wide ribbed sandy plains they swam, following their marine instincts. Over dark seaweed forests they glided. Sometimes they paused to ease the pressure. And sometimes they slowed down to gaze at white jellyfish drifting and dropping through the water like slow-falling silk parachutes.

When they swam through tidal swells, twice the tea-chest slipped off Aquella's back and it took every ounce of Fin's strength to drag it back. Once, in the hazy distance, they saw a shark tear a small fish into tiny pieces with its razor-sharp teeth. Not wanting to be its next meal they took a long route round. Large dogfish, still as stone, hung in the deep water and with their round staring eyes watched the strange spectacle go by. They had seen many weird and wonderful things. The ocean was teeming with them. But a black seal with a crate on its back being helped by a boy was something they'd never seen.

Magnus Fin and Aquella had been swimming for a while, each hoping the other knew where they were going, when they found themselves in the midst of what looked like a coral reef. Fin swept his torch-lights through the water. After the sluggish sights they had become used to it was startling to see bright colour and beauty. It was mesmerising – like a botanical garden at the bottom of the sea. Magnificent plants decorated the ocean floor. Between the bright blossoms of these sea flowers, pink crabs and blue lobsters scuttled to and fro.

We might be close, Aquella said. Fin could hear the exhaustion in her voice. He dived and wriggled himself under the crate, trying to share the load, but no sooner had he done this than the crate slipped to the side.

It's alright Fin, Aquella said, *it won't be long now. Such beautiful gardens have to be King Neptune's.*

Fin brightened his eye-beams, and in the sweep of white saw the silvery figure of Miranda weave in and out between long arms of swaying sea grass. She drew close and nodded in greeting.

I have told Neptune you are on your way, she said, twisting round to join them. She slipped under the crate and helped Aquella, sharing half the load. Fin, still grasping the treasure chest above, felt the speed increase. As though they were the three wise men from the east bearing gifts, they advanced, and even the curious dolphins veered off course to give them room.

We are close, said Miranda, splaying her flippers and gazing down. *Look!*

They looked. They gasped. Their eyes swept in wonder along a curving avenue of majestic brightly coloured plants. As they swam along this path, luminescent jellyfish played their tendrils on giant shells and their muffled music ushered the treasure bearers along.

The avenue led to a mighty rock archway, decorated with a million white clam shells. A solitary and beautiful mermaid sat by the archway, playing on a small clarsach. She had long black hair that reached to her feet. As the two seals and the boy approached she sang softly, and plucked the watery strings of the clarsach.

Fàilte, she sang, *you have returned the Seudan to our beloved Mer King. Fàilte. Fàilte. Ceud mile fàilte.*

Awed to silence the travellers glided through this archway to finally enter the cavern of the great King Neptune deep under the sea.

A mighty conch shell trumpeted. The deep call alerted every creature that swam, crawled and coiled in the cavern. In moments, fish, crabs, lobsters, jellyfish, dolphins, porpoises and eels formed a file of welcome. With Magnus Fin holding the crate in place, paddling his webbed toes gently to propel him forward, and with Aquella and Miranda below, balancing the crate on their strong seal backs, Neptune's stolen treasure made its way to the throne of its rightful owner. As the procession glided by, the onlookers bowed, or nodded, or clicked their pincers together. Each – in the manner of his kind – bade them welcome.

I told them. I said we could rely on Magnus Fin. And see – I was right.

Fin paused for a moment to look in the direction of the voice he had come to know. The tiny pink crab paddled through the water and landed on Magnus Fin's shoulder. *As you have looked after us, we'll look after you. May good winds, good tides and dear King Neptune bless you and yours all your days!*

And with that the crab paddled off and landed on a swinging seaweed frond that trailed from the great cavern door. As though the little crab commanded it, the cavern door, with a thunderous boom, swung open. Emerald-green water gushed and frothed, ushering the travellers in.

From the pounding froth Magnus Fin saw the mighty form of King Neptune rise from a tangle of seaweed and ocean plants. A face full of kindness, at once like the green sea, then like a breaking wave, emerged from the tangles. Neptune's beard seemed like a forest of kelp. His eyes like deep oceans. But Fin, who could only stare into the immense emerald eyes, saw sadness there too.

The mighty Mer King seemed to fumble for a moment. He plunged his great green hand into a tangle of fronds and brought up his three-pronged fork, his Triton.

So much has been taken from me. So much has been stolen. So much the sea has suffered. There has been so much taking – taking – so much greed.

The Triton fell limp in the Mer King's hand, like a wand that could weave no more magic. Neptune rose up from his mighty shell throne and shook his forest of hair. The ocean heaved with him. A million bubbles frothed green and white. In the watery turmoil Miranda slipped out from under the crate and swam up to the king.

Beloved King, Manannán, she said urgently, *Magnus Fin here – and Aquella – have brought back the Seudan. There has, dear King, been much taking as you say, but there has been much giving. Look, look what they bring to you.*

Aquella slowly lowered the heavy crate and slipped out from under it, as Neptune's helpers took it from her back and carefully removed the kist. Exhausted she hung motionless in the water. Fin glanced down and saw the mark from the crate on her back. Neptune too saw it. He stretched out a hand and laid it gently on Aquella's back.

When Neptune spoke, waves boomed and sang. *You have your seal skin returned to you, in good condition I see. I hoped my mending spell had reached the false king's ruined palace before my powers failed me. From this distance, I couldn't be sure.*

Oh, thank you, King Neptune. It was Magnus Fin who found it, she said, the exhaustion gone from her voice. Aquella spun in the water, showing off her beautiful seal skin. *And it is perfect.* She sounded radiant again, and full of life. *Magnus Fin found the stolen treasure and the key. He has brought the Seudan back to you.*

Then Magnus Fin found his voice. His words were few but they rang like pounding waves. *It was a group effort,* he said.

The best kind of effort, said Neptune. *And now...* he turned his deep gaze upon the metal chest *...that which was stolen from me, you say, has finally been returned.*

A hush rippled through the cavern as King Neptune reached his mighty hands towards the kist, which now lay on a stone stand. Slowly, with trembling fingers, he lifted back the lid and a brilliant rainbow light flooded the cavern. In that moment the sadness was swept from his eyes. The jewelled light that shone from the box lit up the swirling water and stretched far. It lit up the avenue of flowers. It lit up sunken ships. It illuminated vast tracts of water. It lit up the bay. The light from the Seudan lit up the whole sea.

All shall be well, said King Neptune, the radiant light shining in his eyes, his face, his whole being. Then he looked at Magnus Fin, this special child who had been sent from the land to help the creatures of the sea. *Choose one*, said Neptune, extending his magnificent green hand towards the treasure chest. *You too carry the sea's wisdom.*

Magnus Fin chose a small emerald stone and slipped it into the pocket of his wetsuit.

Use it wisely and it will bring humans good fortune, said Neptune, *as you from the human world have brought good fortune to us.*

Then King Neptune plunged his hand into the sand below his throne and brought up a small golden coin. *And this*, said the great sea king, laughing kindly and extending the glinting coin, *in the currency of the land, will buy you a new wetsuit and perhaps a little more.* And his laugh rang out. It cleaned the seas. It refreshed the tides. It healed the fish.

All the way back to the bay, Magnus Fin, swimming between Aquella and Miranda, heard the echo of that laughter. They all heard it. It spurred them on. It carried them to the rock door. Miranda swam back to the selkies in the bay. Aquella slithered onto the beach. And Magnus Fin grasped the shell handle, and pulled. He raised his head above the surface of the water and breathed air in the way of humans. Then he hoisted himself up onto the ledge of the high black rock.

For a while Magnus Fin stood, gazing out to sea. The blue water shimmered and the sun glinted upon the surface, like a million golden coins.

He stretched out his arms and breathed deeply. The sea was his. The land was his. As he shook out his hair and lifted his arms to the sky he felt like the richest person on earth.

"Fin!" Aquella shouted from the mouth of the cave. "Let's see if they left us any sausages!"

"Good idea!" he called to her. "I'm starving!" And he jumped down from the high rock. As he scrambled over the skerries and leapt over rock pools he wondered how many sausages he could buy with a golden coin.

Hundreds? He leapt over a high rock.

Thousands? He scuffed up a tangle of seaweed and kicked his heels in the air.

Millions? He turned a cartwheel in the sand.

Yes! Magnus Fin guessed that with the sea king's golden coin he could buy whatever he wanted!

Chapter 33

Mrs Anderson was chuffed that Billy Mole, whom she'd come to see as a kind of grandson, said he was staying on for a few more days, if that was OK with her? Never had she seen such a change in a person. He was polite. He ate porridge. He helped with the washing-up. And when he stood awkwardly in the living room one evening with a sheet of paper and a pen in his hand, she sat down and helped him write his last piece for *Inside Lives* magazine. Mrs Anderson's spelling was a good deal better than Billy Mole's.

Dear Boss and Gaza and Si

Sorry, but I won't be coming back. I have decided I don't really want to be a journalist. I think I am going to travel a bit - see the world, you know - might even sail the seas. I want to do something good. Live a bit. I came up here looking for aliens and you know what I think? Well, I think we're all different. And I think that's alright. And I think it's good to meet different people. I hope I haven't let you down too much and hope you get on OK with the magazine, and I hope you find

somebody else to make the tea. So anyway, that's all from me.
  Yours sincerely
  Billy Mole

There was a lot of letter writing going on in the far north of Scotland. While Lorelie was busy making solstice party invitations for the selkies, Aquella made invitations for the land folk. She gathered lots of the loveliest shells from shell beach at John O'Groats – whelks, Venus and clam shells – then set about writing the invitations in her tiniest handwriting on bits of paper no bigger than her thumb.

Come to the midsummer party
where the land meets the sea.
9pm – summer solstice –
past Ragnor's cave

When each invitation was written she rolled up the paper and pressed each one into a shell. There was one for Barbara and Ragnor, one for Tarkin, one for Billy Mole, one for Mr Sargent and his wife, one for Granny May. Of course there was one for Magnus Fin. And because the shell invitations looked so beautiful, Aquella gave one to herself. She stood it on her windowsill, counted down the days to the party, and sewed white cowrie shells on to her green dress.

Under the sea, Lorelie plucked strands of green, red and pink seaweed and plaited them into necklaces, long enough to circle the neck of a seal. On each necklace she wove in two shells. This, in the selkie way, meant a wedding would be celebrated. It said: *Please come and join the party*. There were shell necklaces for Miranda, Shuna, Coll and Sylva, Catriona and Louise, Ruiraigh and Shannon, Ondine and Don, Eirinn and Rob, Rondo and Maura, Erla and Lachlan.

And when the sun made its journey on the longest day, all would be there, casting off their seal coats and taking on their human forms. On the beach past the cave they'd meet with the land folk to dance, feast and sing.

Lorelie counted down the tides until her wedding day.

Seven... six... five... four... three... two...

One!

It was midsummer's day. The sun rose at three o'clock that Sunday morning. Granny May arrived at the cottage down by the shore at nine and spent the whole day helping her daughter with the baking. Barbara made the pizzas, the sausage rolls and the sandwiches. Granny May took care of the sweet things – the chocolate cakes, cupcakes, fairy cakes, millionaire's shortbread and strawberry tarts. Magnus Fin spread the chocolate on the cakes, placed the strawberries on the tarts and decorated the cupcakes with blue and green wavy icing. Aquella spent most of the day singing, washing dishes and folding napkins. Ragnor was down at the beach gathering driftwood and setting it ready for a bonfire.

In the early evening a sea mist rolled in, which Granny May said was a big shame but the selkie members of the family just shrugged their shoulders, as if they knew something she didn't.

By eight o'clock that evening Magnus Fin, in his new blue trousers and red T-shirt, led the way along the beach path, carrying all the sausage rolls. Aquella followed, carrying the strawberry tarts. She wore her beautiful green bridesmaid dress that she had decorated for the occasion with a hundred white cowrie shells. In her long black hair she had threaded tartan ribbons. As she ambled along she hummed a tune.

Granny May wore her cowboy hat, jeans and her fringed suede jacket and carried her cakes. She hoped there would be some country and western music.

Barbara, who walked to the beach beside her, with her guitar slung over her back, said it could possibly be arranged. She carried a picnic basket filled with everything she could think of – paper plates, cups, juice, marshmallows and macaroni pies!

Ragnor was down at the beach already, setting out stone seats, hanging garlands of sea grass around the arched entrance to the cave, and making sure the beach was free from litter.

Still the sea mist clung to the coast like a silver curtain.

While the food was being set out on stone tables, Ragnor lit the fire and the dry wood crackled. The blue smoke spiralled upwards and was lost in the mist. Magnus Fin took ten of the best sausage rolls, ran over the skerries and threw them into the sea. The selkie party wouldn't be the only party that night. He watched as the flaky pastry sunk downwards. Was it his imagination, or did he see a flash of silver hooks jostle under the water? *Happy solstice,* he called out, and was about to turn and head back to the beach, when he heard the unmistakable yelp of a seal. Black and silver heads rose from the mist-covered sea. Fin whipped out his penny whistle from his back pocket and played his tune of welcome.

The seals slithered onto the rocks. Fin played on as more and more seals, honking and calling, hauled up onto the land. Barbara had joined the tune with her guitar while Ragnor blew softly through a conch shell. Howling joyously the seals rocked and bounced over the skerries and up the beach. Still the mist swirled. It sat like a blanket over the seals, shielding them as they burst from their seal skins and took on human form. It was only when they ran – now as boys, girls, men and women, dressed in glistening outfits of red, gold and green – that the sea mist lifted and the midsummer sun burst through.

With the lifting of the mist curtain the other guests arrived. Some came laughing and cheering. Some came shyly and softly. All were dressed in their best and all carried gifts: food, drink, wood for the fire, drums to bang or rattles to shake.

There never was such a party. Tarkin joined Barbara on guitar and everyone danced. They danced in circles, they danced in pairs, they danced in the shallow water, they danced on the sand. Even Billy Mole danced. In between dances he told Magnus Fin and Tarkin how Mrs Anderson had helped him find a job on a tall ship, helping disabled people sail round Britain. Then the music started up again and Billy Mole danced with Shuna, then with Erla, then with Granny May. "This," he said, to everyone he met, "is the best party ever."

When the conch shell announced the wedding celebration everyone put down their cakes, their drums, their sausage rolls and ran to the water's edge. Ragnor had been softly blowing the conch shell. Now he stepped out from the cave, looking, thought Barbara, as handsome as the day she had met him, at this very shore, thirteen years before.

And if Ragnor was handsome, leading the selkie bride and groom in a slow procession along the shore, Lorelie and Ronan were even more so. It was Granny May who broke the awe-struck silence of the watching crowd. "Isn't she a bonny bride?" she said and everyone nodded. She was.

Lorelie wore a long dress that appeared woven, not from human threads but from threads of Neptune's jewels. It shone red, purple, white and gold. An emerald crown sat on her head and her long black hair, threaded with tiny cowrie shells, cascaded down her back. Ronan wore a suit of red, purple, white and gold. Again it was Granny May who just couldn't keep quiet. "Really gorgeous outfits," she said with an admiring sigh. "You don't get clothes like that in our shops, do you?"

By this time Ragnor had led the bride and groom close to where the excited guests were gathered. As a hush of expectation fell, Miranda stepped out from the group of guests, with Aquella by her side. "We're going to get the service now," Granny May nodded, telling everyone what was going on.

"Is this a normal Scottish wedding?" Billy whispered.

Magnus Fin just winked, smiled and said, "Yeah, it's a Scottish wedding, but it's not normal!"

"Ace!" Billy whispered, and he might have said more but Miranda at that moment invited the bride and groom to stand, with one foot each in the water and one foot on the land. Then Aquella sang the beautiful Gaelic *Dan Nan Ron* – the song of the seals, that she had been practising for weeks. As she sang Lorelie and Ronan exchanged wedding necklaces. And when the song ended Ronan and Lorelie, gazing at each other, chanted the selkie wedding charm:

You are my wind on the wave,
My joy in the water,
My quiet on the rock,
My strength in the hunt,
My friend, my mate, my love.

As they spoke the last words of the blessing a glistening emerald wave curled around their ankles. The selkie couple looked down in wonder. The playful wave gently withdrew, leaving the soft webs between their feet shining. King Neptune had come to the wedding, and blessed them.

Then Ragnor blew the conch shell once more, the sign for Miranda to cast an offering of sand into the sea. Then, addressing Lorelie and Ronan, Miranda sang the selkie wedding blessing:

May bountiful tides be yours,
May pure seas and peaceful coves be yours,
May land and sea afford safe sweet haven,
And in the selkie spirit of the ages,
To each other be kind.
Be true.

Then Aquella threw the confetti and as it fell about them everyone cheered, clapped and whistled. Coll played a wedding reel on the chanter, and the happy couple hugged then danced on the sand.

Selkies love parties and especially weddings. Later, when feasting resumed and the guests were gathered around the great bonfire, Ronan made a speech, saying if it weren't for Magnus Fin he'd still be stuck in a fridge at the bottom of the sea. Then Lorelie made a speech, saying she would love Ronan till all the seas gang dry. Ragnor said a few words about how he hoped there would always be peace and love between selkies and humans. During his speech Magnus Fin, Aquella and Tarkin all turned and looked at Billy Mole, who winked at them, put his thumb in the air and smiled.

Later Mr Sargent sat on a stone with Billy Mole. "I never said fish boy," he explained. "And I never used the word alien; I just want to set the record straight. I was simply curious. The truth is that Magnus Fin has taught me more than I've taught him; I'm sure of it. Aquella too, and Tarkin. We're all different – in our own way – don't you agree?"

Billy Mole nodded his head. The very idea of calling anyone fish boy seemed like a dim, distant and bad memory. Then Barbara whisked him off to dance, and while they were dancing she told him there *would* be a Spain after all, there would be paella and Flamenco, there would be a holiday, because Magnus Fin had brought home a golden coin. Then she laughed, spun out her long red hair, twirled round then gasped. "What's that?" she cried, staring out to sea.

But Tarkin had already seen the yacht in the distance. He'd been toasting a marshmallow on a stick when he spied something out at sea, moving through the flames. His oozing marshmallow drooped into the fire. Tarkin staggered to his feet and ran down the beach. He leapt onto the rocks and scrambled over the skerries. The yacht, its white sail shaking, was heading into the bay, clanging its bell. Flapping at its prow Tarkin saw the unmistakable red, white and blue of the Stars and Stripes, and leaning over the side of the yacht and waving wildly was a man. And not just any man.

"Dad!" Tarkin yelled. "Dad!" and he jumped into the sea.

Magnus Fin heard the splash. In moments he was on his feet. He leapt over the rocks. In disbelief he stared at the blond head of Tarkin bobbing up and down in the water. "Dad!" Tarkin yelled again.

Magnus Fin bent his knees. He was ready to plunge in after him, when he saw Tarkin's arms arch and scoop through the water. Tarkin was swimming!

Tarkin swam all the way to the yacht, which by now had dropped its anchor. A tall, sun-tanned man with long hair and a red scarf tied round his head urged him on. "Son," the sailor called, his voice choked with emotion, "my son!" and he threw a rope ladder over the side.

Fin watched with a lump in his throat as Tarkin mounted the rope ladder, swung his legs over the rail and fell into his father's arms. Fin wasn't the only one watching. The whole party had run to the tideline and there they stood, waving and cheering.

Much later that evening, Carl, Tarkin's father, sat by the fire telling everyone the story of his great Atlantic crossing: "You may think I'm a mighty strange one, believing in magic," he said, looking around him at the attentive faces glowing in the firelight. "But I swear a mermaid guided me. She pulled me through storms. She set me on course. She guided me round rocks. And when it got lonely out there on the open sea, she sang to me."

A tear glistened in Carl's eye. He hugged his son, who was beaming uncontrollably, and nodded at the company. "It's true," he went on, "every bit of it." Everyone around the bonfire smiled at the man who had crossed the Atlantic Ocean. They patted him on the arm. They shook his hand. But no one thought he was mighty strange.

Encouraged, Carl carried on, "I swear she brought me right here, right to my boy. I couldn't have done it on my own." Carl put his arm around Tarkin's shoulder.

Later, as the sun went down, Tarkin, leaving his father talking with Ragnor and Barbara, wandered over to sit beside Magnus Fin. The two of them polished off the last of the chocolate cake.

When the cake was done they wandered onto the rocks. The North Star came out. Tarkin coughed, winked and, like a magician, stretched out his hand. Nestled in the palm of his hand something glinted.

"It's true about the mermaid," he said. "She found them. She said these pearls helped her find me, and now Mom can have them back. Can you believe it, Fin? She's here! She found me. And she brought Dad all the way over here."

Magnus Fin shook his head in amazement. After all their adventures, on the land and in the sea, this seemed the most remarkable of all. Magnus Fin watched as Tarkin carefully pocketed his mother's pearls then turned to gaze out to sea. "She's out there, Fin! See that white frothy wave?"

Fin nodded. Not far from where the yacht was anchored he could see a playful foaming wave.

"That's her," Tarkin said confidentially. Then he turned to Magnus Fin. "I told you, didn't I, Fin? I always knew one day she'd find me. Dad too. I just knew it!" For a while the two friends were silent. The water lapped by the rocks.

On the beach the fire burned as darkness fell. Tarkin, with drooping eyes, sat beside his dad, tired now after the wonders of the day. His sleepy head lolled against his dad's chest. The fire crackled.

Later the embers glowed as the sound of laughter and song turned to yelps. A few seals slithered from the dark cave and with a splash slipped into the sea. Ragnor stood at the water's edge and waved to the departing selkies. The midsummer party was drawing to an end as Magnus Fin walked over the skerries and sat alone on the black rock. He played his penny whistle and watched as one by one the remaining seals returned to the sea. The moon had risen and its pale, almost ghostly light lit up a pile of shimmering sea clothes, discarded by the water's edge. Fin heard a soft deep call. He looked out to the moonlit sea and saw Miranda's silvery head lift from the water. She gazed at Magnus Fin.

All shall be well, she whispered. *Thanks to you, dear child of both worlds, the Seudan and the skin are returned to their rightful owners.* Then Miranda, the selkie queen, sank below the sea.

Still Magnus Fin sat peacefully on his rock, letting one foot trail down into the cool water. He would sleep soon, and dream of this party and of all that had happened. He looked up suddenly, startled at the sound of a soft splash. He fixed his gaze on the water ahead. The dark water ruffled, then a beautiful black seal, shimmering in the moonlight, rose from the water. With her green twinkling eyes she gazed at him. Fin's heart thudded in his chest. "Aquella!"

Magnus Fin, she said.

Fin gasped. "Don't go!"

I am not gone, she said kindly, *only changed.* And with a slow curve of her tail fins Aquella slipped beneath the water.

Change, after all, was something Magnus Fin understood. He wasn't afraid of it. He would see his cousin soon.

Mgnus Fin watched the sea. Stars came out. Behind him he heard the murmured voices of people around the embers of the fire. He smelt the wood smoke and breathed in deeply. He'd be twelve years old soon. He'd go up to high school. And it would be good – he knew it would. There was so much to learn, so much to do.

The words of Miranda echoed on inside him: *All shall be well.* The wisdom of the ocean was restored. The selkie secret was safe. And he, half selkie, half human, could see his selkie family any time he wanted.

For a long time Magnus Fin stayed on the black rock, with one foot dangling in the cool water, then he went back to join the others around the fire.

A Guide to the Selkie Tongue

In the past there were many more selkies. They were frequent and much loved visitors amongst the good people of the northlands. They wandered easily amongst the Gaelic-speaking peoples of the Highlands and the Western Isles and not surprisingly learnt their tongue. But nowadays there are very few selkies, and likewise not so many folk speaking Gaelic.

The selkies related to Magnus Fin came originally from the Western Isles but when their way of life was threatened they moved to the remote island of Sule Skerrie in the Northwest Atlantic. After many quiet years there they longed again for human company. Intrigued by the people of Caithness, a band of selkies travelled around the north coast, eventually settling in a bay close to the shore down the rugged coastline between John O'Groats and Dunbeath.

Though the selkies communicate chiefly by song, pitch, honks, howls and barks, they can also speak Gaelic and English. Language comes easily to them, though their favoured language is music. In this book there are a few Gaelic words. Overleaf are translations and guidance on how to pronounce these words.

Ciamar a tha thu – pronounced *Cimar a haa oo* – How are you? (singular/informal)

Ciamar a tha sibh? – pronounced *Cimar a ha shiv* – How are you? (plural/formal)

Ceud mile fàilte – pronounced *Kee-ud meela faal-che* – a hundred thousand welcomes

Fàilte – pronounced *Faal-che* – Welcome

Seudan – pronounced *Shay-dun* – Jewels

Tapadh leat – pronounced *Tapa lat* – Thank you (informal)

Tapadh leibh – pronounced *Tapa liv* – Thank you (plural, formal)

Tha gu math – pronounced *Haa gu ma* – I'm fine

Tioraidh an-dràsta – pronounced *Cheery an draa-sta* – meaning bye-bye, or, as we say in Scotland, Cheerio!

Acknowledgements

A lot of people – and places – have helped me in the creation of Magnus Fin and I'd like to thank them here.

Firstly I'd like to thank that far-flung, wild cliff, beach- and sea-ringed county of Caithness in the far north of Scotland. I'd also like to thank the Scottish Arts Council, Northlands Creative Glass and Lyth Arts Centre for bringing me to Caithness as a writer in residence in 2006. I had never been that far north before and was astounded by the quality of light, the expanse of sky and the ever-changing mystery of the sea. I'm sure, had I not lived so close to the sea and in a place with so few distractions, Magnus Fin would never have managed to find his way into the pages of three books.

Caithness and Sutherland retain a sense of wilderness, and in such landscapes it is easy to set the imagination alight. So thank you Scotland's northlands, thank you the village of Dunbeath – in particular the beach, the cave, the skerries, the seals that visit these shores and the seal pups born on those stony beaches. Thank you to the seal pup born close to my house and well done you for hiding under the upturned boat during the storm and managing to rock and roll over the rubbish strewn on the beach to make it to the sea. Thanks to everyone who cleans beaches and encouragement to those who don't. Thanks David and Rosemary for allowing me to stay in Neil Gunn cottage. Thanks John Irvine for taking me out in your boat. And heartfelt thanks also to all the good children of Caithness.

Thanks to my uncle John – an artist – for encouraging me, a long time ago, to jump into his old pool thick with frogs and slime. And not only to jump in – but to swim! Magnus Fin is always taking courageous jumps and my uncle John, I suspect, inspired that in me.

There are many other people who, in different ways, have helped me and who I'd like to thank. Firstly I would like to thank all my family for being creative, artistic, persevering and for encouraging that in me. I would like to thank Davie Calder and Megan, for patiently listening to great chunks of Magnus Fin and for offering me insightful feedback. I'd like to thank the people at Brownsbank for offering me a short residency in Hugh McDiarmid's cottage to complete this book. I'd like to thank my agent Kathryn Ross for, anonymously, offering wonderful feedback on what became the first book, and for her support since. I'd like to thank my editor Sally Polson for her imaginative and invaluable editing skills. I would like to thank all the good people at Floris Books, and may Kelpies continue to flourish!

I'd like to also mention a few dear friends who have given me encouragement and support over the years by following their own creative star – and by showing an interest in mine. Thank you David Campbell, Catriona Murray, Lorna Hoy, Fergus McDonald, Sharron Tweedale, Andie Lewenstein, Louise Coigley, Marjan Broers, Joan Docherty, Amber Connolly, Jean Luc Leirritz, Michel Syret, Nina Naesheim, Rupert Jenkins, Shuna Anderson, Lynne Mahoney, Donald Smith,

Alexander Mackenzie, all my wonderful creative-writing students – and last but never least my wee collie dog Flora who has had more walks by the beach than any dog I know. And apologies to the many dear friends not mentioned here by name.

I would also like to say a huge thank you to the hundreds of children I have met while visiting many schools, from Shetland to Sussex. Thank you for sharing your own stories – and thank you for reading Magnus Fin.

Janis Mackay

Janis Mackay

Author Interview

Q. How did you become an author?

Janis Mackay [JM]: I've always liked writing. I have written poems and short stories and had them published, but I suppose being an author means having a book published. *Magnus Fin and the Ocean Quest* is the fourth book I wrote for children – but the first to be published. So I suppose winning the 2009 Kelpies Prize made me an author!

Q. What inspired you to write the Magnus Fin *series?*

JM: I used to live by the sea. One day I was walking along the beach and saw a few dead seals. I also saw a lot of rubbish. And I felt so sorry for those innocent and lovely creatures who live so close to us and have to suffer because of our rubbish.

Q. Who is your favourite character from the Magnus Fin books?

JM: At first I think Tarkin was my favourite. He is very free and unusual and quirky and I like that. Then Miranda was my favourite in a mystical selkie way. But I have to say Magnus Fin. He is a bit shy but he is also brave. He is sensitive and cares about animals – and he wants to enjoy his life and make a difference, not hurt people.

Q. How long did it take to write Magnus Fin and the Selkie Secret*?*
JM: Quite a long time. I wrote the book, then re-wrote it, then wrote it again, then edited it, then edited it again. Probably a year in all.

Q. How do you decide what the cover of your book looks like?
JM: I think Nicola Robinson (the illustrator) is wonderful. I love her covers. I like the covers to be stories in themselves – so by looking at the cover you get a real sense of what the story will be like. For this cover I thought it would be good to have Neptune's treasure chest, and Magnus Fin in the cave.

Q. The Magnus Fin books are full of cool sea creatures. Which one is your favourite?
JM: Of course I love seals. I live close to them and have seen them on the beach as pups. I have looked into their eyes and heard them sing. I watch them swim.

Q. Magnus Fin's friend Tarkin can't swim. Is there anything that you can't already do that you'd like to learn?
JM: I'd like to sing well, cook a good meal, climb mountains, and speak fluent French. There are lots of things I can't do, but I also know it takes a lot of practice to do certain things – like play the piano for instance. Mostly I want to write really well, and that I suppose is what I practise most.

Q. What is the best thing about being an author?
JM: There are lots of wonderful things. One is creating characters who come alive. Although I spend most of the day on my own writing, I feel I am in great company. Another wonderful thing is meeting children for whom Magnus Fin and the gang are real.

Q. Do you plan your stories in advance?
JM: When I first began writing I didn't know what the next sentence would be until I wrote it nor did I know what was going to happen next. I think that is a good way to write, especially when you are just beginning. I plan a little bit now and try to strike a creative balance between planning and being spontaneous. Writing is an amazing thing. You can plan clever things, then somehow as you write, the story tells you to do something else. That is why writing is exciting.

Q. Magnus Fin is half selkie. If you could be any supernatural creature, what would you be?
JM: An angel!

Have you discovered the Discover Kelpies website?

Adventure
Animals
Environment
Friendship
History
Laughs
Legends
Magic
Monsters
Secrets
Spooky
Thrills

Discover Kelpies is *the* website to visit if you love books!

- Read all about your favourite Kelpies books and authors
- Check what is happening on our blog
- Read exclusive extracts of new books
- Enter competitions
- Discover new books in your favourite subjects whether you love adventure, animals or magic!

How can *you* get involved?

- Sign up to our Discover Kelpies eNewsletter

- Send us reviews of your favourite Kelpies books

- Take a quiz, write your own story or make a wish with our Fun Stuff page (new fun things are being added all the time!)

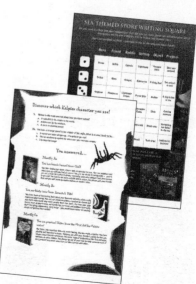

Log on now at
discoverkelpies.co.uk

The Magnus Fin books are also available in eBook format.

Janis Mackay

Join half-selkie hero Magnus Fin on two exciting
underwater adventures as he struggles to save the sea
and his selkie family.

Winner of the Kelpies Prize 2009.
Magnus discovers he is half selkie
-- part seal, part human -- and
must find new courage to save the
ocean's creatures from an evil force.

When Magnus Fin discovers his
initials scratched into the rocks
by the shore, he knows his selkie
family need his help and an
exciting adventure begins.

Lari Don

Helen and her fabled beast friends face treacherous tasks and dangerous monsters in three thrilling adventures.

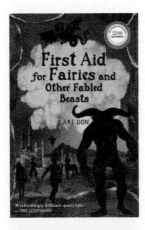

First Aid for Fairies and Other Fabled Beasts

Wolf Notes and Other Musical Mishaps

Storm Singing and Other Tangled Tasks